Time for Terri

Also byRoslyn Bane

The Long Way Home

Time for Terri

Roslyn Bane

Desert Palm Press

Time for Terri

Smoky Mountain Romance Book 1

by Roslyn Bane

© 2015, © 2019 Roslyn Bane

ISBN-(trade) 9781948327107
ISBN-(epub) 9781948327114
ISBN (pdf) 9781948327121

Desert Palm Press
1961 Main Street, Suite 220
Watsonville, California 95076
www.desertpalmpress.com

Editor: Mary Hettel
Cover Design: Michelle Brodeur (eebooWORX)

Printed in the United States of America
Second Edition February 2019

Acknowledgement

First edition acknowledgments

Special thanks to Anson Barber for all the encouragement and advice you provided, and for taking time out of your own busy writing schedule to beta read for me.

Thank you to Andrew Grey for the excellent advice on writing same-sex couples.

To the folks at Patton Veterinary Hospital, thanks for your assistance and encouragement.

To the highly-skilled instructors at the Nantahala Outdoor Center who made learning to kayak a great experience and loads of fun, I can't thank you enough.

I have tweaked the geography of Bryson City and the other towns mentioned to fit my demands.

Second edition acknowledgments

Thank you to Danielle Z. and AJ Adaire for your advise on the story, and to Mary Hettel for editing.

Special thanks to Lee for accepting the book for a second publication run so the series could continue.

DEDICATION

With Love to Family

"Do you believe in something that you've never seen before?
Oh there is Love. There is Love."

Peter, Paul & Mary

Chapter One

"MORNING MS. GREENE, HOW was your trip? Where'd you go this time? Let me help you with that." The chubby young teenager rattled off his questions without seeming to take a breath, picked up one of the boxes, grunted a little with the weight of it, before settling it into his arms.

"Thanks, Jimmy. That's a little heavy." Terri almost grabbed for the box as it tilted but stopped as he regained balance. She easily hefted another box of similar size. "My trip was great, I went to Australia. I was in Melbourne, Sydney, and spent a few days up in North Queensland."

"Did you see any kangaroos?"

Terri opened the passenger side door of her dark green jeep, set the box on the floor, and stepped aside as Jimmy loaded the other box onto the seat. "As a matter of fact, I did. I'll show you the pictures sometime. Do you still work in the library after school? I'll come down later this week."

"I do. Thanks." Jimmy smiled as she handed him a folded bill. He turned to walk away, and then looked back. "Welcome home, Ms. Greene."

Terri finished her errands and headed back home, driving leisurely and with a smile on her face as she passed the familiar sites. Her head snapped to the right as a blur appeared, she hit the brakes hard and grimaced when there was a sickening thump followed by a sharp yelp.

"Shit!" She pulled over and ran back to the animal.

"Oh damn." She pressed a hand to her stomach as it roiled. A wave of nausea rushed through her at the sight of the mangled leg and blood. The yellow Labrador retriever lay whimpering, its eyes glazed. "Oh, poor baby."

Terri ignored the gravel biting into her knees as she knelt and placed a hand on the dog's chest. The fur was coarse and matted with dirt and briars. Its ribs were prominent, and the dog's heart was racing. Looking around for help, and seeing no one, she ran to the car, grabbed her jacket and an old towel. She raced back to the dog, stroking its head, keeping her voice soft she whispered, "Come on, let me help you." She wrapped the coat over the dog's head and it started to fight. "It's all right, hold on." She lifted it quickly, then set it back down on the towel, wrapping it tightly. She carried the dog to her Jeep, placed it inside, and sped back toward the veterinarian's office. "Please be open."

Spraying gravel as she turned into the parking lot, she beeped her horn and was relieved to see a woman come out. "Is Doc James here?"

"No. I'm the new vet, Sheila McDevitt. What happened?" She glanced into the back of the jeep and saw the dog. "Let me get a cart, we'll bring her inside."

Terri stroked the dog's head again and looked into its brownish yellow eyes, remembering her long-gone childhood dog. She whispered to it, her voice calm and soothing, "You'll be okay." She wondered when the tall blonde vet had started at the clinic.

Lifting together they placed the dog on a cart. "It ran out in front of me. I couldn't stop in time. I tried to miss it."

"Let's get her inside. We can talk more in there." The vet wheeled the cart back across the parking lot while Terri hurried ahead to open the door. As they moved through the corridor to an exam room the dog whimpered and tried to rise but was easily held down. Together they positioned the dog on the exam table. The dog yelped and started to shake. Terri stood by quietly as the doctor listened to the dog's chest and abdomen with her stethoscope. "Her heart and lungs sound fine. The belly is rumbling like it should. This is good." Using a penlight, she checked the dog's eyes and then looked in its ears. "Good, the pupils are reacting to light and there is no blood or fluid in her ears."

"What does that mean?" Terri asked.

"It means there is probably no head injury."

The vet looked up. "So far everything else looks pretty good. I'll do a more detailed exam later, but I want to give her something for pain before I exam the leg thoroughly. Will you stay with her? Keep her on the table while I go get the medicine? My staff is not here right now."

"Of course." Terri petted the dog's head gently and stroked between its eyes until the vet returned. She watched as the doctor cleansed the leg and injected the medicine. After a minute the dog's eyes began to droop. Terri stood by watching as the vet continued to examine the Lab. The woman's voice was subdued, calm and soothing. The dog visibly relaxed as her hands moved over it. Terri watched as the vet carefully examined the leg. With great care she moved it, causing the dog to whimper and try to pull away. Terri noticed the woman's brow furrow as she continued the exam.

The vet turned to Terri. "I'm afraid I can't save the leg. I can remove it, or I can put her down."

"What? No! Is she okay otherwise? You would kill her because she's hurt?" Terri heard the anger in her own voice and tried to calm herself.

"No. Sorry, let me explain. Other than the leg injury and some bruising the dog will be fine. But a lame dog can have a very hard life. The dog appears to be a stray, certainly it's not well cared for. It can't be left on its own."

"No. She ran out. I've never seen it around town. Does it have one of those chip things?"

"I'll check." The vet ran a wand over the dog, scanning. "No, it doesn't."

"I guess I have a dog then."

Sheila paused. "That's very nice, but Ms…"

"Terri, Terri Greene."

"Well, Terri, I don't want to dissuade you, or seem cold, but the cost of care and the difficulties of a lame—"

"I want the dog. Do what you can."

Sheila nodded. "This could be quite expensive."

Terri hesitated, for a few seconds. "What's expensive?"

"Offhand, it's going to be close to twelve hundred dollars, maybe more."

Terri swallowed. "Whew. That is steep." Her heart dropped as she looked down at the dog and saw its pain-filled eyes staring at her. Her breath stuttered as she decided. "That's okay, go ahead."

"Let me make some phone calls and get one of my assistants back to help me."

After several minutes the vet returned, her eyebrows wrinkled "I'm unable to reach my staff. They both had plans to go away this weekend. I can sedate her more. Make some other calls."

"What do you need? I'll help."

"I don't think that would be appropriate."

Terri set her jaw "I don't care. I can hold things, reach for things. Tell me what you need."

"It's not only that, it can be quite disturbing if you're inexperienced."

"So is watching something suffer. Please." Terri watched the vet, saw her frown and her mouth tighten as she considered what to do.

"Okay. Stay here with her and try to keep her calm, I'll get things set up."

***

Ninety minutes later, Sheila sat dictating her examination of the dog, and then the operative notes. She glanced occasionally at Terri, watching as she sipped the cold water Sheila had given her. The woman had done remarkably well and had only needed some gentle reassurance a few times to help steady her. Her brown eyes were very expressive and had revealed her emotions and distress during the surgery.

"Hey, Doc?"

Sheila looked over and smiled. "Yes?"

"I think in the excitement I forgot your name."

"Sheila McDevitt. How are you feeling?" She saw a faint blush rise on Terri's cheeks. It stood out in sharp contrast on her still pale face. Slender, with a smoky voice, her high cheekbones and narrow face were fascinating. Despite her obvious discomfort, the woman was stunning.

"I'm okay. Sorry I got a little queasy in there." Terri rubbed at the scar on the back of her hand. "You were right, I've never seen anything like that before."

"You did fine. That's why I put a chair in there, so you could sit down if you needed to. You were a tremendous help. I couldn't have done it without you." She glanced toward the sleeping dog. "You're giving her a chance. Most people would have left her lying in the road."

"I couldn't do that. I had a dog that looked like her a long time ago." Sheila noticed the darkening of Terri's eyes, heard the tightening of her voice.

"You must have cared for it very much."

Terri looked up, nodded. "So, when did you take over here?"

"About six weeks ago. Dr. James was retiring. Instead of him having to close the practice, I bought it from him. How long have you been coming here?"

"Actually, today's the first time. I only know him from around town.

"Seems like everyone knows everyone."

"Bryson City is pretty small. Where are you from? I'm guessing the Mid Atlantic area?"

Sheila answered, "Northern Virginia, born and raised."

4

"What brought you here?"

Sheila tapped her pen against the table and hesitated, trying to decide what to reveal to a client. She nodded her head slightly, "Starting over. Divorced."

"Sorry about that. What brought you here, though? Small towns can be tough for outsiders."

"Tell me about it," she muttered. "I wanted to go out on my own. Work with both large and small animals. Go someplace my services were needed."

Terri glanced over to the sleeping dog, the only animal in the place. "Well, she's a large breed anyway. Business will get better as they get to know you. Did you keep the staff?"

"Yes. But if business doesn't pick up—"

"It was a good idea. They're your best advertising right now. They'll keep the regulars up to date. From what I've seen, folks will come around soon enough."

"Thanks. So, are you in advertising?"

Terri laughed, a rich, deep, throaty laugh that Sheila found surprisingly sexy. "Oh, hell no! I could never sit around all day making gimmicks and jingles. I'm a photographer." She looked over to the kennel when the dog started to whimper.

"She's becoming more alert, and is confused and scared, but she's not in pain." Sheila went over, spoke softly to the dog, checked how the IV fluid was running, and made some adjustments.

"How soon until she's fully awake?"

"I'll keep her lightly sedated until tomorrow. Then we'll see how she does. She'll need to stay here for a few days. I would like to see her weight start to come up. Plus, I'll need to do more vaccines, check for disease, parasites."

"Do what you have to."

Roslyn Bane

Chapter Two

TERRI SAT IN THE nylon camping chair, her boot-clad feet now noiseless in the gravel parking lot of the overlook. A million stars were bright in the moonless sky and the smell of the damp woods enveloped her. She breathed in the earthy smell of wet leaves, soil and water, and smiled. She listened as the sounds of the woods returned now that she had stopped moving around to set up her photography equipment. The skitter of small animals along the ground, the call of owls seeking their mate, a coyote yipping—the sounds that once scared her—now they were as welcoming as a lover's embrace at the end of a long day.

She shivered and reached down to open her thermos, the scratch of the metal as the lid turned was barely above a whisper. Breathing deeply, she enjoyed the heady aroma of the dark, rich coffee, and the puff of warmth across her chin as she blew on it. She sat and sipped, patient as light started to appear in the east. About twenty minutes, she thought, and she could start shooting the sunrise. Until then she would watch and listen, enjoying this moment of solitude.

The outline of the surrounding mountains started to appear in more detail as the sky lightened. She rose, stretched, and moved to her camera, the animals of the woods instantly quieting. The gentlest of breezes rustled the leaves, and carried the now familiar scent of dogwood, flame azalea, and rhododendron.

The smells and sounds of the mountains disappeared as she viewed the world through her lens, the sound of the camera shutter not registering. The sky brightened with red-orange as the sun came closer to the horizon, until at last it erupted above the mountains. A ball of fiery red painted the sky with color and cast a surreal pink glow over the clouds snaking their way through the valleys and over the mountain tops that gave the Smoky Mountains their name. *God, I love this place.*

***

"Sheila, there's a dog in the back. It wasn't here yesterday morning.

What happened?" asked Jamie, Sheila's veterinary assistant.

"Yes, the poor thing was brought in yesterday afternoon. She got hit by a car. Unfortunately, I couldn't save her leg. She'll be here a while until she gets stronger."

Jamie looked at the log for the billing information. "This says Terri Greene."

"Yes, she brought the dog in."

Becky, the clinic receptionist interrupted. "The mysterious Terri Greene brought in the dog?"

"Why do you say mysterious?" Sheila questioned.

"She's lived here for over five years and doesn't get out much."

Jamie replied, "Oh, stop it. She does, too. True, she doesn't come to every town function, but she travels a lot and probably wants to chill out in her own space before she hits the road again. I've talked to her many times at the store, at the library. She's very friendly. I went to her show here last year and to another over in Charlotte."

"Her show?" Sheila stopped ruffling through a chart and looked at Jamie.

"The library does monthly shows, displays of local artists' work. Terri had some of her photos on display. I've never seen anything like it. It's amazing. And they're not necessarily pictures of exotic places, but normal stuff around here. I recognized most of the places, but I've never seen them like that. She answered questions, talked to kids. She even showed people how to use their cameras." Jamie's fingers flew over the keyboard, and then she angled the computer screen. "Here, come take a look."

Sheila looked at the images on the web page. "Oh my, they're beautiful. Wow. She didn't say much about what she did. I asked while she was here. She said she took photos. I figured she took portraits at the mall."

The women laughed. "The mall? You're in Bryson City. The closest mall is almost an hour away. You're in the country now, Doc. There is no mall, but there's a big shopping center over in Waynesville. That's about forty minutes away."

Before they could continue, a client came in. Becky checked them in while Sheila went into the back to review the file on her patient.

***

Terri arrived at the clinic at nine-thirty and stood by watching as

Sheila and Jamie brought the dog out of the kennel and into an exam room. The dog whimpered, and Terri pressed her hand against her chest and squinted. "Is she in pain?"

"We gave her some medicine for pain earlier, but she'll be a little sore. And she's afraid. See how her tail is pulled down, and her ears are lowered. So, we'll take our time and let her get used to us."

Sheila spoke to the dog softly. "It's all right, girl. Things are going to get better for you." She placed a small piece of kibble in her open palm and brought it over to the dog who sniffed and gobbled it down. "Good girl."

"She's hungry," Terri said.

"Probably. She is underweight. Who knows when the last time she ate was. Last night she only had fluids." Sheila repeated feeding the dog several times until the dog was lying with its head erect. "Here, Ms. Greene, you can give her a few while I examine her."

Terri stepped forward, placing a nugget of food in her hand and offering it to the dog. She took it fast but with surprising gentleness. Terri watched as Sheila used her stethoscope to listen to the dog's chest and abdomen. "Is everything okay?" she asked as soon as the vet was done.

"Yes, her heart and lungs sound good. Her abdomen is soft and noisy like it should be. Give her a few more of those and then why don't you go stand by the door."

"Okay." Terri did as instructed and watched as the dog tried to stand and follow her. Sheila reached under its belly and helped steady the dog when it swayed. Terri watched as Sheila pressed softly on its abdomen, before stroking along the bandaged leg stump. "She's licking her mouth a lot."

"That's okay. That's what some dogs do when they're hurting. Call her."

Terri looked at the vet. "But she'll fall."

"She will. But not today. I'm going to help her."

Terri stooped down. "Come here, girl. Come on." She held out a piece of dog food. She jumped forward as the dog tried to step and started to fall. She gave a quick sharp exhale when Sheila caught the dog and lifted its hips, bringing the good leg back under its body. She looked at Sheila. "You're making me tease her, she's going to fall."

"No, you're not teasing her. I am going to help lift and steady her, so she starts to learn what to do and gets stronger. You're helping me and developing a relationship with her at the same time. She wants to come to you. That's what we want. We'll do it a few more times and then I must check the wound. You don't have to stay for that."

"I'd like to."

"You did well yesterday, you'll do well today." They worked with the dog for five more minutes until it lay down and refused to budge. "Stay here with her. Give her some loving. I'll be right back."

Sitting on the floor Terri ran her finger on the soft fur between the dog's eyes, smiling slightly as the dog sighed and stared at her. "What's your name girl? Where are you from?" The corners of her mouth curled up when the dog rolled onto its side and showed her belly. Terri started to scratch it and the dog thrashed side to side on its back. "Does that feel good? You like that, don't you?"

Terri and the dog were startled when the door opened, and Sheila and Jamie entered. "We're going to lift her up on the table to look at her leg." Terri stepped back out of the way and watched as Sheila lifted the dog from the side and Jamie held its head. They positioned her on her side. Sheila nodded at Terri, "Come talk to her."

Terri stepped forward and spoke softly to the dog, stroking her head while Sheila and Jamie removed the bandages. "Is everything okay?"

"Yes, it is. Do you want to see?"

Terri scraped her teeth on her bottom lip, "I think so. It can't be worse than last night, right?" She looked into Sheila's eyes for reassurance and saw kindness and compassion.

"That's right. Remember we shaved it down so there's not too much fur by the end. The sutures are holding so it's not bloody. It is a little swollen, but it has a nice healthy pink color."

Terri swallowed hard, and bit down on her lip lightly before looking at the leg. The air rushed out of her lungs as she looked at the stump "It doesn't look bad. I mean, I don't know what it's supposed to look like, but it's not...um...too gross."

Terri's stomach flipped when Sheila smiled. "It looks exactly like it's supposed to. Now we'll show you how to clean it, and the next time the bandage needs to be changed, if you're here, you can help. You'll need to inspect it daily for several weeks to make sure it's healing well. If it starts to ooze, smell funny, or she starts to lick at it a lot, we need to see her."

"Okay." Terri watched as Jamie wiped the wound with a gentle soap, applied an ointment, and then re-wrapped the stump with gauze and vet tape. Jamie explained the steps as she was performing them, and when she was finished, rewarded the dog with another piece of kibble.

Sheila lifted the dog down and held onto it with firm hands as the dog struggled to find her balance. She looked at Terri. "If you have time, I want you to help get her outside. Stay behind her and if she starts to fall, support her under the belly so she can balance herself. She needs to build up her strength in the other leg and as that develops her balance will get better."

Ten minutes later, Terri was outside, sitting in the grass while the dog lay next to her panting. "Oh my God, that was tiring. I can't imagine how exhausted she must be."

Sheila handed Terri a bottle of water. "You were bent over a long time. That gets hard on your legs and back."

"That's for sure." Terri sat up and took a long drink. "How long do you think it will be before she figures out how to walk?"

"She knows what she has to do now. She just needs to get stronger. It will be a few days before she will be able to come out here without stopping to rest on the way. It's likely she will forget a few times and fall. It's important to make sure she doesn't reinjure the leg when it does happen. I'll keep her here until she's stronger and healthy. We're going to feed her a special diet for the next few days. It will be higher in protein, since she is underweight. It will help her build muscle."

"Okay. Do you mind if I come down again later today?"

"Not at all. She needs to get to know you. Come over whenever you want. We open at eight and close at five or five-thirty most days. I will come by in the evening and check on her again before it gets too late."

"Thanks. I'll be by later this afternoon." She stood up, offered her hand to Sheila. "Thanks so much, Doc." She looked at their joined hands when she thought she felt a tingle.

"My pleasure." The doctor smiled again, and Terri felt a flutter in her abdomen.

Terri stopped by the clinic twice daily spending time with the dog in the yard. The yellow lab was doing better at attempting to walk, albeit with a slow, awkward, hopping-style gait and would tire easily. Terri would help her get up from a lopsided sitting position to standing, and when the dog grew tired, she sat on the ground with her, petting her. She brushed her coat daily and checked the dog's leg, cleaning and dressing the wound herself. Slowly they began to bond.

***

Sheila watched the two of them through the window whenever she had a chance. Terri was very patient as she reviewed basic commands with the dog and praised her when she responded as well as the injury allowed. It was obvious that the dog had some basic training, but Terri was improving on it. She saw that Terri's hands were always gentle, her voice reassuring.

Sheila began to wait to examine the dog until Terri was there because she asked many questions about the dog's health. Sheila felt a growing fondness for the intriguing owner. She'd looked at Terri's website several times, going through the galleries. Her outdoor photos were breathtaking and conveyed a variety of moods. She marveled at the photos of ordinary things that somehow became alive and vibrant. In her mind she tried to reconcile the Terri she saw in the clinic with the skilled photographer who appeared to travel the world. Becky was right; Terri Greene was somewhat of a mystery. She always spoke to Jamie and Becky, asking them questions about their families, and neighbors. But Sheila noticed she never shared much information about herself other than answering their questions concerning her work.

The office had no clients scheduled so Sheila sent the workers home with an apology that there was no work. She stayed, reviewing invoices, looking at food and medication supplies, trying to find better prices. One afternoon, a week after the surgery Terri arrived for a visit and the dog whined excitedly as she approached. Sheila smiled. "She is becoming quite attached to you."

"I hope so." Terri turned and looked at Sheila.

"Let's go outside. It's too nice to stay in here. I want to see how she's doing with walking, and I have a few questions for you."

They went outside, walking slowly as the dog hobbled in a slow, jumping gait. They watched as the dog moved around the fenced area. "She's doing quite well, and her strength is coming back. I think you may be able to take her home soon. She is eating plenty, and her weight is coming up. You'll want to be careful not to overfeed her. With her not being able to run it will be easy for her to get too heavy, and that will make it even more difficult for her to get around. Do you have a fenced yard?"

"No, I don't. Do you think she'll wander?"

"I don't know. Some dogs who have been on their own do keep

that wanderlust in them and will always roam if given a chance. I don't think you'll have that problem though. She realizes she is vulnerable. She also realizes she can trust you. I've been watching you." Terri looked over, her eyebrows raised in surprise. "You are very good with her. Very patient. I feel good about you leaving with her. I know you will take good care of her."

"I plan to."

"Have you decided what to name her?"

"I've been thinking about that but haven't decided yet. I want something that fits her."

Sheila smiled. "I understand that. I did want to talk to you about having her spayed. Even though she may not wander, males will come for a visit. A pregnancy would be very difficult for her as she picks up weight."

"I imagine so. Well, it needs to be done. I certainly can't handle a house full of puppies, and I think this one has enough challenges already. When can you do it?"

"I'd like to give her another day or two to recover. She still has difficulty pushing up to stand sometimes. After the surgery she will be a little sore and I wouldn't want her falling over and ripping open the sutures."

"Okay."

"I have some more work to do, I'll leave you two to your training session. Come inside and let me know when you want to leave."

"Sure thing." Sheila watched as Terri walked back over to the dog, noticing the gentle sway of her hips, and the view of her very shapely ass. She shook her head to clear the surprising thought.

***

An hour later Sheila was immersed in a spreadsheet when Terri came back in. "Sheila, do you have a minute? I need to ask you something."

Sheila looked up, met Terri's gaze and found herself mesmerized. She had never thought brown eyes interesting, but Terri's brown had specks of green in them, and her gaze was unusually direct but not unsettling. Sheila had seen such compassion in her eyes when Terri had initially worked with her to help the dog. She had the feeling that Terri Greene could look at someone and know immediately what was in their soul.

"I have a business proposition for you. I frequently travel for my business. Sometimes I'm gone overnight, a couple times a year for several weeks. I would like you to consider if I could leave the dog here while I am away. But not in a cage. I don't want her locked up all day. I would pay you, of course. The normal kenneling fee, plus the cost of any lost business because she would stay here overnight. I would also pay an additional fee that we could negotiate for your time and effort."

"How much time are you talking about?"

"Over the past twelve months I've been out of the country eight weeks and had another ten trips that lasted up to a week which were out of commuting distance." When Sheila hesitated, Terri continued, "I couldn't leave her to die, but I can't give her the home she deserves. At least not without help."

"This is very unusual. Do you want her roaming free here?"

"I would prefer that, and the fenced area outside is ideal, weather permitting. If there are problems with other animals, then she could be caged..."

"Kenneled."

Terri smiled. "Kenneled, while she is here."

"Let me think about this. I need to check the regulations too."

"I understand. So how are you adjusting to town?"

"Ah, well, I am definitely an outsider."

"Give them a little time. Get out and socialize a little."

"Everyone seems friendly enough but somewhat wary."

Terri laughed. "They'll get used to you and vice versa. Where have you been?"

"The usual. The grocery store, post office, and hardware store. Some young boy keeps trying to help with my packages."

Terri smiled. "That's Jimmy. Nice kid." Her expression sobered. "They're going through some hard times. His father is a disabled vet. He got injured in Iraq, lost his legs. He works from home doing computer consulting. His mother left, she couldn't handle the changes. Financially, they're struggling. Jimmy helps by doing odd jobs. He's not old enough for a lot of hours. People usually give him a tip when he helps them. It's something we started doing. They won't take handouts."

"That's good to know."

"So, have you been anywhere else?"

"I've been out to some of the riding stables."

"Oh, that's called getting settled and drumming up business. How about a night out?"

"No, I haven't."

"You need a night out. Would you like to go to Natasha's Bistro tonight?"

"There's a bistro here?"

"It's a little place down by the river. The business drops off in the winter, but it's spring now and the tourists will start coming in. It does quite a business."

"A real bistro?"

"Natasha grew up in France and came over to spend a year in the States, but never went back. She married one of the local farmers. Their produce is organic. In the winter their greenhouse supplies most of the vegetables they use. She is quite the cook. It's very nice."

Sheila hesitated. "I need to—"

"Do your errands tomorrow. You need something other than business."

"All right."

"How about seven? We can meet down there. I'll jot down directions for you."

As Terri wrote down the directions, Sheila ran her hands through her hair, "Ah, I feel ridiculous asking this but, what's the dress attire?"

"Definitely not Northern Virginia fancy, this is casual. A couple times a year they do dinners where it's coat and tie. Dresses. You need a reservation well in advance for those. They do it so people can have a nice night out for special celebrations. A couple of the churches have gotten in on it and have overnight kids' nights with pancake breakfasts the next day." Terri laughed and met Sheila's gaze. "There is nothing like a kid-free night and sex to make everyone happy."

Sheila felt her cheeks start to burn and mumbled, "I imagine so."

6

Chapter Three

TERRI STOOD IN FRONT of her closet, suddenly unsure of what to wear. She'd been to Natasha's several times with friends and neighbors. But this seemed different. Terri was surprised at the sense of relief she had felt when Sheila agreed to dinner. For God's sake, just pick something, it's not a date.

She finally chose a crisp, white cotton shirt, leaving the top buttons open; a gray pair of trousers, and a lighter gray vest. She replaced her simple gold studs with small gold hoops, put on her normal barely-there makeup, and added a touch of light pink gloss.

Arriving at the bistro early, Natasha and Terri spoke in French to each other. Terri fumbled occasionally, and Natasha corrected her, as was their agreement. Terri noticed that the pictures on the wall had been rearranged to fill in some gaps. "It looks like you could use some more photos. Anything in particular you would like?"

"The pictures of the waterfalls are always good sellers. Do you have any of vineyards though? I've seen some you have in black and white of the countryside. Those remind me of my childhood village."

"I know I do. I'll stop by next week and bring the files. You can show me the ones you want, and I'll have them framed as soon as possible. You still get ten percent of the sale."

"Terri, that's too much. You help me decorate the place and pay me to do so."

"No, really, it works for me. You display my work year-round. I don't have that kind of time to show people the pictures and wait for them to decide. Here people can look unrushed and think about whether they want to purchase something. It's fair."

"Fine, but the wine tonight is on us." Natasha led Terri to a table. "Who will be joining you, so I can bring them over?" Before Terri could answer, Sheila arrived, smiling broadly.

"Hello. I'm Natasha, welcome." Natasha pulled Sheila's chair out for her. "Terri, I will bring your favorite wine." She handed them both menus and walked away.

"This looks nice. I took a moment out front to look at some of the paintings and pictures she has up. They're stunning. And the plants are so lush. She's used them effectively to give everyone privacy."

"She does. Did you have any problem finding it?" Terri's eyes flickered over Sheila's body. "Nice outfit." The black pants were well tailored and were paired with a sleek-fitted black camisole that revealed a modest curve of breast. It was topped with a yellow, short-waist summer blazer.

"Thank you. I wasn't sure if I was on the right road. It went on a long way before opening into the parking lot. We're close to the river?"

"It's about twenty-five feet below us. There's a good view from outside, and Natasha has a gazebo right next to it. Those tables are already taken though, so we'll be inside. There's a walkway along this stretch of the river, that connects the businesses with a nice cobblestone path."

"This is fine."

Natasha came back and opened the wine. After offering a sample to both and having it approved, she filled their glasses and returned to the kitchen.

They looked at the menus and after a minute Sheila spoke. "Everything looks so good. Why don't you order, since you know the place?"

"Do you eat seafood or red meat?"

"I do. I'm not a big tofu fan."

Terri laughed. "Well, that's good to know."

When the waitress returned, Terri ordered their entrees, and then topped off their wine. "How are you adjusting to life in a small town?" Terri asked.

"It takes some getting used to. I mentioned a shopping mall the other day at work and the ladies almost fell off their chairs laughing."

"I imagine so. I tend to shop online, or when I travel, I hit the shops I prefer then."

"You mentioned before that you travel. Where have you been?"

"All fifty states, most of the Canadian provinces, Brazil, Australia, and New Zealand several times. I had just returned from Australia the day before I hit the dog."

"I didn't know that. Do you have a favorite place?"

"Right here."

Sheila's eyebrows arched, and her lips parted.

Terri laughed. "Don't look so surprised. I fell in love with the area the first time I saw it. I was out camping and kayaking for a week. I knew I would be back, but I didn't intend to move here. It just worked out that way. What's your favorite place?"

"I would have to say the beaches along the Mediterranean coast. I don't know that I have a favorite one. My parents loved to travel, and they made sure when we went on vacation we learned something about the culture and to appreciate the local cuisine. I've been to Europe several times. A couple of whirlwind tours to get a taste, then dedicated trips to explore more."

The waitress returned with their Soupe au Pistou. "Tell me about your family." Terri spooned up some soup and smiled as the rich aroma wafted up.

"My father is a retired family practice physician, and my mother still works part-time in real estate. She says she'll never give it up completely because Dad would drive her nuts being around all day. I have a sister who is finishing law school and a brother in the Marines." She tasted the soup. "Oh, this is good."

"Where do you fit in there?" Terri asked.

"Oldest. My sister is twenty-eight, two years younger, and my brother is twenty-six."

"Where is he stationed?"

"He's recently returned from Iraq. Two tours. He's getting out in a few months. Thank God. Don't get me wrong, I'm proud of him. I'm glad he's home safe. He wants to go back to school and become a psychologist."

Their entrees arrived: Parmesan crusted organic chicken with risotto, artichoke, and basil lemon butter for herself, and Trout a la Meuniere with asparagus and morels for Sheila. They ate several bites, enjoying the flavors.

"Do you have any pets?"

Sheila wiped her mouth with a napkin. "My ex was adamant about not having pets. It wasn't that way at first but after my cats died, there was too much arguing about it when I wanted new pets. As soon as I get settled a bit more, I will adopt one or two of the strays. Right now, things are a bit too unsettled."

"When did you decide you wanted to be a veterinarian?"

"I don't remember ever wanting to do anything else. I was always bringing home strays and taking care of them. I have always loved animals. My dad finally called a halt to bringing home animals when I was thirteen and we had four dogs, three cats, and a cockatiel. I was

19

hiding them in an old carriage house on the grounds."

"It sounds like a big place." Terri liked the way Sheila's eyes brightened as she spoke of the animals and her family.

"It is. It wasn't in great shape when they bought it, but they fixed it up. I don't recall a time there wasn't some repair or remodel occurring. I remember sometimes when I was young the workers would let me pound a few nails in. It was so exciting at the time that I was 'helping' do the work. But enough about me. What about you? You don't have quite the accent of a local."

"I moved down from Virginia about seven years ago, I've been here for five years."

"So, you're from Virginia? What part?"

"I was in Roanoke for a couple years." Terri shifted in her seat, pushing back ever so slightly from the table, tugging gently at her earring.

"Is your family still there?"

Terri glanced down at her plate and tried not to fidget. Her muscles tensed, and a wave of heat washed through her body. She took a long sip of wine and when she looked up she saw a puzzled look on Sheila's face.

"I'm sorry. I didn't mean to pry."

Terri shrugged. "You're not prying. I believe they still live in New York. I left at eighteen and never looked back. I started by heading south to where it was warmer. Eventually I ended up here. Where did you go to veterinary school?"

"Texas A&M. I met Peter, my ex, down there. When he finished his residency, we moved back up to Virginia. The rest is history. When did you get into photography?"

"I always liked taking photos and drawing. I was able to take a photography class in high school, a few more when I was in Virginia, and finally a couple of professional level courses once I got down here."

Sheila sipped her wine. "What did you do in Virginia?"

"Restaurants, house cleaning, dog walking, drawing caricatures...you name it, I probably did it. I got a lucky break and landed a pretty good job at a brickyard. I was able to make enough money there that I could stop doing some of the other stuff. That gave me the time to take a few college courses. My boss at one of the restaurants wanted pictures of the food and drinks so I took some. They were good enough for him, so he paid me. A few other places wanted photos done, so I studied, and got better. Looking at those photos now I cringe." Terri gave Sheila a quick smile and motioned for the waitress. "Would you like dessert? They always have something chocolate-y delicious."

When the waitress arrived, Terri looked at Sheila "Do you mind if I order again?"

"No, I don't mind."

"We'll have the fruit tart and chocolate sampler, along with the demi sec Riesling."

They finished the meal with Terri filling Sheila in on some of the local attractions and more colorful locals. After splitting the tab, they walked down to the river and listened to the folk musicians that were entertaining the outdoor guests.

Over the next two hours they strolled along the riverfront. The elevated boardwalk ran along several blocks of waterfront. Local restaurants had tables set up for outdoor dining and a few shops that were still open and had their doors open hoping to entice passersby inside. Music emerged from within several taverns as bands played for the customers crowded inside. They browsed through the local art museum and Terri introduced Sheila to people she recognized from around town. Finally, they returned to the parking lot. "You know how to get back to your place all right?"

"Yes. Thank you, Terri. It was good to get out."

"I hope this didn't throw you behind too much with your unpacking."

"I needed the break. I'll be in the office early tomorrow to check on the dog by eight o'clock. Come by if you'd like to see her."

"I'll be there, I want her to start hearing her name."

"Which is?"

"Tripod."

Sheila laughed, a soft sensual laugh, which sent shivers along Terri's spine. "Of course, the photographer's three-legged dog. Perfect."

Terri watched as Sheila drove away. She stood lost in thought for several moments. Sheila McDevitt was quite an interesting woman. And sexy as hell. She'd caught herself more than once looking at her mouth, wondering what her lips would feel like, how she would respond to a kiss. She had to consciously refrain from looking at her cleavage. Her gorgeous breasts were tastefully on display, the curve enticing. *Were those large breasts sensitive or could they take rough handling? Damn!* She had to stop. The woman was divorced, straight. She would not be interested in Terri in that way. Trying to have a friendship with this woman would be challenging.

***

Sheila sat sipping herbal tea, trying to settle in for the night. Terri Greene was a fascinating woman. She'd enjoyed the evening with her but found it hard to pay attention sometimes during the evening. Terri's eyes captivated her. Her brown eyes with the green specks were so direct, so observant. At times, the green in them seemed to flare and become more intense. She had noticed Terri's gaze flick over her body appreciatively and remembering it now, she felt herself start to get aroused.

Even if she admitted it only to herself, she was attracted to the woman. She had imagined herself kissing Terri more than once that evening. She had become distracted several times by her laugh and found herself focused on Terri's mouth. Her lips with the faintest shimmer of pale gloss looked soft and enticing. She had to deliberately stop herself from leaning in and kissing her when they were down at the river, and again in the parking lot.

It had been years since she found herself sexually attracted to a woman. She had women friends, but she had not had a female lover since before she met Peter. She had known she was bisexual since she was a teen. Comfortable enough with the label that when she started going out with Peter, she had told him, believing honesty was the best policy. Other than a few poor jokes about having a threesome—which they never had—it was never an issue.

Now here was an undeniable attraction for Terri. And if she wasn't mistaken, there was some interest on Terri's part, too. But she didn't need the distraction of an intimate relationship right now. She had to get the business on a better footing. She'd already moved past keeping strictly to a client-patient relationship with Terri. After all, she needed friends in the area and Terri was certainly friendly and interesting to be around. Yes, she would encourage a friendship, but she would have to be careful to keep the friendship strictly platonic.

Chapter Four

TERRI JOLTED AWAKE, HER own cry echoing in her head. *Damn. Get out of my head, you bastard. This is my dog.* Her room was starting to brighten with the approaching dawn, and she rolled over glancing at the clock. *Five-thirty? The clinic doesn't open for almost three hours.*

She tried to will herself back to sleep for a little longer and finally gave up. With a sigh and a long stretch, she got up and slipped on some running gear. She spent a few minutes warming up and went outside for a run. An hour later she arrived back home and showered quickly.

Feeling butterflies in her stomach, she picked at her breakfast and laughed out loud at herself. *Calm down, you're like a kid in a candy store.* Restless, she paced the room and moved to the closet. She pulled out the new dog bed and placed it in the corner by the fireplace. She pulled new dog bowls out of a bag, washed them, filled them, and then placed them on a small waterproof mat on the floor. With that done, Terri went upstairs to her office and started to work with constant glances at her watch. No surprise that at exactly eight-thirty she arrived at the vet clinic to bring Tripod home.

Becky greeted her with a friendly smile. "Good morning, Terri. Today's the big day."

"It sure is. I'm looking forward to getting her home. I've wanted a dog for a long time."

"Well, she sure is a sweetie. You've done a lot of work with her. She's more than ready to get out of here. You can go ahead into Room One. Jamie will bring in Tripod in a moment. She was getting a bath and nail trim this morning and should be finished soon."

"Okay, thanks."

A few minutes later Jamie brought Tripod into the room. The dog hobbled over to Terri and greeted her enthusiastically. After several ear shattering barks, the dog quieted and sat leaning against Terri's legs. Sheila came into the room and the dog barked again and wagged its tail energetically.

"Well, she's very excited today. How are you doing?"

"If I had a tail, I think it would be wagging just as fiercely."

Sheila laughed. "Well good. Are you set up at home for her?"

"Yes, I have a bed out for her. I have a few toys and the bowls are filled waiting for her."

"Good, let's go over her medication. Here are some pills. This is an antibiotic and she needs to continue taking it for another two weeks, twice a day. It's for the Lyme disease she has. I'll check her in a couple weeks to make sure the infection has cleared up." She picked up a rectangular box and showed it to Terri. "This is a heartworm preventative. It's once a month. She should have her next dose in two weeks. There are little stickers inside to put on your calendar if you need a reminder, and the directions are on the box."

"What's in the other green bottle?"

"That's a steroid. The dosing is on the bottle. That's to help the swelling go down in the leg stump and it's also helping with the inflammation from the Lyme's. There is enough for one more week. After she finishes it you may find that she doesn't eat or drink as much. That's normal. She doesn't need more than three cups of kibble a day. Give her half in the morning and half in the evening. If there's food left in the bowl when she walks away you're giving her too much."

"Okay. How long do I have to keep checking her leg?"

"Every day for the next few weeks. It doesn't have to be covered anymore but if you see her licking at it you better take a good look. If she falls onto it, of course you need to look."

"That makes sense."

"So, are you ready to take her home?"

"I am."

"I want to say, I've been very impressed with what you have done for her and the time you've already spent with her. If you have any questions or concerns don't hesitate to call. Oh, and let me know when you need boarding. We'll be able to take care of her when you travel."

"I will."

"Well, let's get you two out of here."

Together, the three of them walked out to the jeep. Terri pulled a travel kennel out of the back, and after some gentle persuasion and a dog treat, Tripod climbed inside. Sheila and Terri then lifted her into the back of the jeep. Terri closed the tailgate and accepted the bag of medication from Sheila. Their hands touched for a moment and a quick zip of electricity passed between them, their eyes holding for several seconds.

They reluctantly pulled away from each other when Jamie and Becky came out and said goodbye to Tripod and to give her some new chew toys. After a few more minutes they headed home.

***

Over the next several days Terri and the dog adjusted well to each other. Both awakened periodically in the night with bad dreams, and the other would provide solace and comfort. Tripod was persistent in her efforts to come sleep in the bedroom with Terri, but she was resolute in not letting the dog sleep in her room or come in her office. Tripod would sit or lay patiently waiting for Terri, and on more than one occasion she let out a groan of canine frustration with her restrictions.

After one such loud groan, they went outside and walked slowly around the wood line. Suddenly Tripod stood alert and very still, her head cocked to the side listening.

"What do you hear, girl?" Terri listened for several seconds before she heard the slow steady crunching of a car working its way up the final rise of the gravel road. She stood and waited, wondering who would be coming up. From the sound of the car she knew it wasn't any of her neighbors.

After several more seconds, a dark blue BMW appeared, Sheila's car, and the realization brought a quick jump to her pulse. Tripod barked several times, but stood steady next to Terri, not leaving her owner's side.

Sheila pulled into the short driveway, parked next to Terri's jeep and emerged. Tripod stood whimpering with excitement but remained with Terri. Looking down at the dog, Terri spoke. "It's Sheila. Go say hi. It's okay." The dog moved at a steady pace to greet her other friend.

"Hi. I hope you don't mind me dropping by. I looked up the address from the file. I wanted to see how you both were doing."

"We're doing great. Out for a little exercise." Terri looked over at the beautiful car. "You didn't bottom out coming up the road, did you?"

"No, but I think it was close a few times, so I kept it slow. I was hoping no one would come down at the same time."

Terri laughed. "It gets a little close, and sometimes the pickups have to fold their mirrors in. It can be a real son-of-a-bitch if it's been raining or after a snow."

"I think I know why they call it Broken Rock Road. Some of those exposed rocks look like they were split in two by a giant axe. They're beautiful."

"They are interesting. Would you like to come in, or are you in a rush?"

"That would be great." Sheila stopped petting Tripod's head and followed Terri and the dog toward the house.

***

"Terri, this is beautiful." The Cape Cod-style home was made with high gloss logs and had a large covered porch. The green metal roof and matching shutters accented the brown log home. The lawn was well maintained, with a few bird feeders on the margin where the lawn met the surrounding woods. A large shed blended into the landscape.

"Does the porch go all the way around?'

"It does. I always wanted a house with a big porch. This place has such an amazing view on all sides, the porch had to wrap around too."

Terri opened the door for Sheila and Tripod to enter. She stood back and watched nervously as Sheila looked around her small home. To give it a larger feel, the home had an open floor plan, with a large living room that was set apart from the kitchen by a built-in butcher-block table. The kitchen was small, but had modern appliances, and she kept it spotless. Like she was taught. The walls held brightly colored paintings, and several pottery items sat on the end tables with mosaic tile inlays that she had purchased from local artisans. A picture of a sunrise hung above the mantel. Her sofa and recliner were in good shape but not new, the leather soft and smooth.

"Where did you find the floor boards?"

"I saved them from the original cabin. They don't shine very well."

"They're a nice touch, it adds a solid feel to the house." Sheila moved over to the fireplace. "I love the fireplace. The stone work is unique."

"I drew what I wanted. I thought the curves were more soothing than traditional straight lines. A local stonemason did the work."

"It's beautiful." Sheila looked at the picture hanging above the mantel. It was a photograph of the sunrise over mountains. The clouds in the valley were a surreal pink as the deep red sun peaked along the ridge. "Is this one of yours?"

"It is. I took that the day after I hurt Tripod."

"The colors are so interesting."

"It was a beautiful morning, worth getting up for. Would you like something to drink? I have wine or tea."

"Tea. Thank you. So, how are you and Tripod adjusting?"

"I think we're doing fine. Although she doesn't like not being able to come into my office upstairs. She lies next to the doorway and whines. She tries to crawl in when I'm not looking but I hear her nails on the floor, so I know what she's up to."

"You have an office here?"

"One of the benefits of being self-employed. I do most of my printing and framing here as well. Would you like to see it?"

"I would love to."

Terri led Sheila upstairs. "How easily does Tripod get up here?"

"It takes her a little while, but she gets here. I was worried the first few times she tried."

Sheila turned and watched as the dog hopped up the stairs. "She is doing really well. You've done a great job with her."

"Thank you. She's good for me. She reminds me to take a break every now and then. The young boy down the road, Tyler, is fascinated by her."

***

Sheila stopped inside the doorway and was as impressed with this area as she was the downstairs. The second floor was one large open space with multiple large windows that brightened the room. A workstation held two computers. A huge work counter ran along the opposite wall and held hand tools and several picture frames. Set off to one end was an exercise area with equipment that looked well used. Two large closets, built in bookshelves, and several old but comfortable looking chairs were at the far end of the room. But what caught Sheila's attention the most were the pictures on the walls, particularly a grouping of charcoal sketches.

"Wow, tell me about the pictures."

Terri led Sheila around telling her brief stories about some of the photos. When they came to the charcoal drawings, Sheila studied them. The four drawings showed a young woman, standing in a meadow, with trees around her. Each picture, although similar in design, had a different mood about it. In one it appeared as if a storm was raging—not only around the woman, but from within her, too. The mood in the second was serene; the third could best be described as utter joy, and the final as thoughtful.

"These are wonderful. So powerful." As Sheila looked at the drawings, she felt Terri's gaze on her. Trying to ignore the sudden tingling that started inside she leaned closer. "Who did these?" She jerked back and looked at Terri. "You did these. My God, Terri, they are amazing. When did you do them?"

"About ten years ago."

"You would have been in high school. Were you not interested in continuing with art?"

She watched as Terri rubbed at her neck, glanced away, and was quiet for several moments before she answered. "It wasn't an option for me."

Sheila looked back at the sketches and studied the face of the woman, she glanced at Terri and back again. "It's you. You're the young woman. There's such passion in these." She noticed the rigid set of Terri's shoulders. "They obviously mean something special to you."

"It was right before I graduated. It was a very exciting and emotional time. Like it is for most high school seniors. I could never bear to throw them out."

"Throw them out? Why?"

"Well I traveled light for a long time. But I couldn't ever let them go. So much of me went into them. My art teacher agreed to hold them until I asked for them. Once I settled down, she sent them to me."

Sheila thought it was curious that her teacher had held them, but then realized she had not seen any photos of family members downstairs. In fact, she had not seen evidence of a family anywhere in the house. She remembered what Terri had said that she left New York at eighteen and never looked back. She spoke softly. "Eighteen is young to leave home. Were you excited to get out on your own?"

Terri flinched at the question. "My parents and I didn't see eye to eye on a lot of things. They were very strict. Tyrants really. I couldn't continue to live with so little freedom. I would have never met their expectations. To have stayed would have killed me a little more each day."

Sensing Terri's unease she changed the topic "You have a nice view from up here."

"I love to look out and see what's around me. The natural light is good for my work too."

"You like the bright, airy feel."

"Absolutely. I hate feeling closed in. Trapped." Tripod whined at the doorway, watching them move around. She lay down and stretched one paw into the room.

"No, Tripod." The dog grumbled and pulled her paw back beyond the threshold.

"I feel bad, but her fur would play havoc with the electronics. I clean my own cameras and lenses. Dog hair would make that much more difficult. I'm hoping keeping her out of here will help some."

Tripod whined again.

"Tripod, let's go downstairs," Terri said and turned to Sheila. "You have to see this."

Sheila watched as the dog slid down the steps on her belly until stopping in a controlled crash at the bottom, then stood up, tail wagging and banging off the adjacent wall. They came downstairs and Terri pointed down a short hallway. "The bedroom is back that way, along with the bath." She pointed beyond the kitchen. "Utility and laundry down there. That's about it. It gives me the space I need without being too much to care for."

Sheila felt a tiny flicker of unexpected disappointment when Terri did not show her the bedroom. "Terri, this is a nice home you have." She pointed to the French doors. "Is west that way?"

"Yes. I like to watch the sunset whenever possible. Helps me put things in perspective. Come look, it's the best view I have from outside."

Sheila went onto the wide porch. A patio table and chairs sat off to one side and several rocking chairs on the other end. The view of the surrounding mountains and valley was magnificent.

Terri pointed. "The sun will set right about there tonight, between those two peaks. In the winter it will drop behind the smaller peak to the left."

"You know where the sun sets by season?"

"If you live somewhere long enough and pay any attention, you'll notice the changes. Would you like some lunch? It's after two."

"You don't need to bother, I just wanted to stop by and see how you two were doing. Oh, and I also wanted to talk to you about something I saw that might help with Tripod."

"Explain it over lunch. If you have time? I was going to grill some burgers, I'll even put some bacon on one for you. I heard you tell Jamie you were craving a bacon cheeseburger."

"I am. You've twisted my arm. How can I help?"

"Just relax, I'll get things together pretty fast. You could walk with Tripod around the yard. Help her get used to her boundaries."

***

Terri opened a small bin, pulled charcoal out, and then lit the grill that was down on the lawn. In the kitchen, she washed lettuce, sliced tomatoes, formed the burger patties, and cooked several slices of bacon. By the time the coals were ready, she was coming back outside at the same time as Sheila and Tripod were coming up onto the porch, the dog carrying a huge stick. Tripod plopped down next to the table while Terri started the burgers. She felt Sheila's eyes on her, turned and caught her gaze. She saw her hazel eyes brighten before Sheila looked away and sipped her tea.

While the burgers cooked Terri answered Sheila's questions about the area's tourism, and what shops were better in the adjacent towns. Finally, the burgers were done, and the aroma of the chargrilled meat wafted across the patio.

Sheila inhaled deeply. "That smells fantastic."

Terri watched as Sheila took her first bite.

"Oh my, this is so good. I've missed having a bacon cheeseburger. There was a place near my home in Virginia that made the best. I know I could make one, but it seems like so much trouble. Moving here might help me beat my junk-food addiction. Although this burger will probably kick it back into high gear."

"I could help you develop all sorts of bad habits." Terri smiled broadly before biting into her own burger.

Sheila laughed. "I did come by to tell you about something I saw that you might find useful for Tripod. They make wheelchairs for dogs. It's a combination of harness and wheels. There are several styles based on whether a front or back leg is damaged. I've requested some information, but it won't arrive for a few days."

"I hadn't thought of anything like that. That would help. I've been worried about how I was going to get her enough activity, so she doesn't get too heavy and have even more trouble getting around."

"I'll call you when it comes in."

"If you like. Or you could come by. If I know when you're coming, I'll make some pulled pork the likes of which you didn't have in Northern Virginia. We'll get you accustomed to a new kind of junk food. Although barbecue is not junk food."

Sheila laughed. "I'll keep that in mind. I don't want to get the locals stirred up."

***

After Sheila departed, Terri sat outside enjoying the quiet as Tripod dozed next to her. Her thoughts drifted through the afternoon. She was pleased that Sheila had come by and stayed for lunch. She thought that several times she had seen an overtly sexual gaze from Sheila, and that she had focused on her mouth repetitively. She had noticed Sheila's gaze drift over her body like an appreciative caress, but then just as quickly the sensation was gone.

Terri smiled, remembering Sheila's comment about getting the locals stirred up. She laughed out loud when she thought that Sheila was getting this particular local stirred up in a very different kind of way. Without any doubt, Terri realized she was very attracted to the lovely veterinarian, and that she had to get her attraction under control before she scared the woman off. If Sheila was interested, if those sexy gazes weren't only in her own imagination, Terri could wait until Sheila made a move.

Chapter Five

NEAR THE END OF the following week Sheila received a large catalog of medical devices used for animals who had leg problems. She reviewed the catalog, compared the items to other products online, circled and highlighted several that would be able to help Tripod. Calling Terri, she agreed to stop by that evening to drop off the material.

Tripod stood on the porch barking excitedly as Sheila walked from the driveway. "Hi, Tripod. Why are you barking at me? Are you happy to see me?" She bent over and ruffled the dog's head and neck.

"She sure sounds like she's happy."

Sheila jumped and yelped in surprise when she heard Terri's voice behind her.

"Sorry, I didn't mean to scare you."

"I didn't hear you come up behind me. Were you around the side?"

Terri gestured across the lawn. "No. I was over in the woods."

"You came all the way over from the woods? I didn't hear you."

"I walk quietly. Old habit. If you want, I can learn to make more noise when you're around. Maybe you could help?"

Sheila felt the heat rise in her cheeks at the suggestion. She had no idea how to respond so she smiled for several seconds. She saw a glint in Terri's eyes and gave a sigh of relief when Terri chuckled and broke the tension. "Come on in. Let's see what these things look like." She opened the door and ushered Sheila and Tripod in. "Would you like something to drink? Maybe some wine?"

"If you're having some, I will."

"Pinot grigio okay? I opened some earlier."

"Perfect."

"Go ahead and sit down, I'll bring it over."

Terri brought over the wine and a plate of cheese and crackers, setting it on the coffee table. "I thought you might be hungry since you're en route from work." She pulled a dog biscuit from her pocket and offered it to Tripod, who immediately plopped down and munched enthusiastically.

"Thank you." Sheila took a cracker and opened the catalog. "I've circled a few things that are the right style and size for Tripod. There are several to choose from, the big difference is how small they fold down to and what the harness material is made of. You'll want something that cleans up well."

They spent fifteen minutes going through the catalog and reviewing the different features. Sheila was aware of the slight tension between them. It was obvious that there was attraction, but thankfully Terri seemed intent on ignoring it.

As they were finishing the review of the material, Sheila added, "If you decide to order, let me know. I can get you a discount. By the way, if you plan on taking her on any trails, you'll want wider wheels for stability."

"I was hoping to. Do you think I could take her swimming? I think it would be good exercise for her."

"Even though it looks like she has gotten stronger since I last saw her I think you should wait a little longer. And you should get a canine life jacket, because she could have a difficult time. She won't get the propulsion that she needs, and her balance will be affected."

"That makes sense."

"Well, I need to get going. Let me know which one you want, and I'll order it for you. Thanks for the wine and cheese."

***

As Sheila gathered her purse to leave, Terri stood watching and not wanting her to go, but having no legitimate reason to delay her departure. She wanted to see her again, but with Tripod on the mend that wasn't likely to happen any time soon. Terri walked Sheila out to her car, hesitating several feet before reaching it. "Sheila, would you like to go hiking tomorrow? There are some fantastic trails all around here."

"I haven't hiked any difficult trails in a few years."

"There are some trails that aren't too severe and have beautiful waterfalls. There's even a few that are handicap-accessible, but I don't think you'll need that. You look like you're in pretty good shape." *Damn fine shape.*

"That sounds nice. I've wanted to start exploring the area more but didn't want to head out on my own."

"Well, now's your chance. How about if I pick you up at nine? I'll pack a lunch."

"I'll be ready." Sheila wrote down her address and phone number. She handed the paper to Terri. "I'm looking forward to it."

***

They spent the day hiking in Dupont State Forest, up to Bridal Veil Falls, and along Grassy Creek Falls. Sheila was patient while Terri took photographs. She watched as Terri rubbed absently at her lip, and wondered how those soft, full lips would feel. *How would the kiss taste?* She shook her head, trying to clear the thought. She wasn't going there. She didn't have the time for an intimate relationship. She wasn't even sure that she wanted one. Having friends to do things with was all she needed.

As they ate lunch sitting on some sunny boulders, Sheila felt desire tug at her several times. She tried to ignore it, but Terri somehow kept her off balance. There was nothing sexual about what they were doing or saying, but the tension was building. Terri regaled her with stories of some of her travels, and despite her efforts Sheila found herself increasingly attracted to Terri.

"Are you ready?"

Sheila jerked up. "Oh, you're finished. I got distracted. Yes, I'm ready. Where should we go next?"

"It's getting late. We need to start hiking back. It will take about an hour if I can keep my camera down. Please tell me to stop if it gets annoying."

"I don't mind. I like seeing you work. I'm trying to see what you see. Will you show me the pictures later?"

"Sure. We should get going." She put her hand on the curve of Sheila's back as she guided her back to the trail.

Sheila smiled at the gentle warmth of Terri's hand on her back as they walked. When Terri moved her hand as they started walking back down, Sheila felt a little twinge of disappointment at the loss of contact.

While driving back to town, they chatted about upcoming local events, their hobbies, and bucket lists. Sheila was surprised that Terri knew a lot about Chinese cooking, could speak several phrases in Chinese, and was fluent in French. They both were avid readers and had read several of the same books, including some from authors not well-known. She had become embarrassed when she revealed that she could play piano and guitar and Terri insisted on someday hearing her play. She was glad she hadn't revealed that she could also play clarinet.

Arriving back at Sheila's house, she invited Terri in for a glass of wine and was a little disappointed when Terri declined, saying she had some work to finish up. She watched as Terri drove away and decided it was best that Terri had left. She needed to think about the feelings she was experiencing and decide what—if anything—she was going to do about it.

Chapter Six

TERRI STOOD TALKING WITH several other artists in the library. The Spring Arts and Craft Show was underway. Indoor paintings, stained glass lamps, sketches, and photos were on display. Outside, the parking lot and town square were filled with craft vendors selling handmade clothing and jewelry. Local vintners had wines for sale. Homemade baked goods were stacked high on tables, and the smell of pork barbecue filled the air.

The library was open and packed as residents came out to admire and purchase the works of their neighbors. Terri, as usual, had a large crowd around her. She talked about her travels and photographs. People asked her about their own cameras, and for better picture-taking advice. She graciously answered questions, thanked people for stopping by, and made the occasional sale.

In midafternoon, as the food judging was underway, the smell of barbecue became stronger and people drifted outside. Pressing a hand to her stomach to suppress the rumble, Terri's eyes widened when Sheila appeared and handed her a plate of food and a bottle of water. "Hi. I didn't know you were here."

"I figured you might be hungry. This barbecue tastes great."

"Thanks for the food. It smells so good."

Sheila looked around. "You've been busy. I stopped in earlier, but you were swamped." Their eyes met and held for several seconds before Sheila broke eye contact. "Sit down and eat. How's business?"

"About what I expected. I had a few sales. I never expect to do a lot. But I like getting out with the locals, giving support to the other artists and vendors."

"I was hoping that you would tell me about what you have displayed after you finish eating."

While Terri ate, Sheila spoke to several people who recognized her and answered questions about pets and products. Terri watched her interactions. The way her blonde hair swung slightly when she moved, a smile on her face as she greeted people. Her soft feminine laugh had her stomach fluttering. Terri watched as Sheila ran her hand through her hair, gathering it and releasing it, her pale neck visible for a second. Terri shifted as her core warmed and she thought about kissing that delicate neck. She startled when she realized Sheila was looking right at her. Everyone had moved on to other displays and they were alone. *God, how long have I been staring?*

"How do you like it?"

Terri's eyes widened, and she struggled to swallow. "What?" she gasped.

Sheila laughed. "The barbecue. How do you like it?"

With heat rushing to her cheeks, Terri wiped at her mouth with the napkin. "It's very good. Tangy. Just the way I like it."

"Tell me about your photos."

For the next twenty minutes Terri spoke about some of the photos and the trips she went on. Terri was acutely aware of her proximity to Sheila. A subtle citrus scent lingered, and as Sheila flipped her hair with her hands, the scent blossomed in the air before fading again. How would it smell with her nose pressed against that flesh, and her tongue licking at the skin? *Get a hold of yourself, Terri.*

Terri thrust her hands in her pockets to keep her from tucking some wayward hair behind Sheila's ear and smiled when Sheila did it herself. They were interrupted by a couple returning to purchase a photo they had looked at several times during the day. Terri discussed matting and framing it for them and completed the sale.

After they departed, Sheila asked, "Would you like to come over for dinner tonight?"

Terri felt a quick flutter in her heart, as a thrill of happiness coursed through her. "I would like that. Thank you."

"When do you finish up here?"

"I'll be out of here by five."

"Why don't you come by around seven?"

"I'll see you then." Terri couldn't help but smile at the gentle sway of Sheila's hips as she walked away.

***

Sheila welcomed Terri inside and graciously accepted the bottle of Cayuse Syrah that she extended. "Terri, this is very nice, but I'm afraid what I prepared for dinner is hardly worthy of a wine like this."

"Put it aside for some other time then."

"Come on in. Did you have any problems getting here? Would you like a drink?"

"No problems, and a beer would be great. If not, wine is fine."

"Is Heineken okay?"

"Yes."

Sheila handed her a bottle and glass. Terri set the glass aside. "Let me give you the tour."

The house had a spacious interior with an open-floor plan. Large glass doors along the back of the house provided an unobstructed view of the mountains. Tan and cranberry walls framed the large living area with ceramic tile flooring. A comfortable leather sofa and chairs were grouped to encourage conversation. A vintage upright piano sat off to one side. A stone fireplace was at one end, and to the left an L shaped kitchen held modern stainless-steel appliances and a sand-colored granite countertop. A dining table was placed adjacent to the glass doors allowing natural lighting. Glossy wood trim ran along the floorboards and ceiling throughout the downstairs. A full-sized bath and large laundry room completed the first floor. A back deck ran along the length of the house.

The upstairs level held four large bedrooms. The master suite held a king-sized four-poster bed, an antique dresser, and matching end tables. A corner fireplace was fronted by a silvery-green loveseat. The en suite had a Jacuzzi tub big enough for two, and a double-headed walk-in shower. A small balcony led to the outside from the master suite and connected to the main level deck by wide stairs. The other rooms were set up as extra bedrooms and an office.

"Sheila your home is beautiful. And the view is fantastic."

"Yes. And even though there are houses nearby, the way they're situated you can't see into anyone's backyard. At my home in Virginia, the houses were so close I swear you could hear and smell your neighbors cooking bacon in the morning."

Terri laughed.

**

Chills traveled along Sheila's spine when Terri laughed. She took a long look at her guest. The fitted blue-linen pants complemented her tan skin, and her slender figure. The sleeveless white blouse exposed her firm, strong arms. *Is her skin as smooth and soft as it looks? Would her long, slender fingers be soft and sensitive or firm and strong?* With a subtle shake of her head, she realized that she had said nothing for several long seconds. "I thought we could eat outside, if you don't mind."

"I don't mind, it's a wonderful night."

"How is Tripod?"

"She's doing well. She was a little upset that I was heading out, she turned her face into the corner when I was leaving."

"Oh my. You could have brought her over."

Terri shook her head. "No, that's not appropriate."

"Well for future reference, I wouldn't mind." Sheila led her out to the deck. The patio table was set with a cream-colored cloth and bright colored plates. Stemware of various sizes were arranged beside each place setting. She gestured to a chair. "Make yourself comfortable, I'll bring out the appetizer."

"Do you need some help?"

"I got it, you can relax and enjoy the view."

***

As Sheila walked away, Terri smiled. She certainly was enjoying the view. The blue scoop neck shirt revealed a peek of Sheila's generous breasts. Her calves, exposed from under sleek black capris, looked strong, and Terri imagined them wrapped around her. Her hips swayed enticingly, a smooth rhythmic motion that Terri wanted to experiment with. She was smiling as Sheila returned. "That looks delicious."

Sheila placed the bowl of colorful salad with white meat down alongside a plate of tostadas. "It's ceviche, a marinated fish."

Terri sampled the dish. "Oh, that's good...really good."

"I'm glad you like it. It's a favorite of mine in the summer." Sheila sat and was immediately captivated by Terri's eyes. Suddenly nervous she dragged her teeth across her bottom lip and took a sip of her wine. "How was the rest of your day?"

"It was enjoyable. I sold a few more prints. And turned down two requests to photograph weddings."

"Really? You're not interested in that?"

Terri shuddered. "Not in the least. It would be a cold day in hell before I did that."

Sheila broke into a wide grin with the look of horror on Terri's face. "I don't blame you."

"I noticed you had a few people stop and talk to you about their pets. That's good."

"They did. I hope they consider what I said. Nothing sounded serious, but their dogs need to be checked."

"If they're smart, they'll bring them to you." Terri took a sip of her beer. "So, of all the places you could have practiced, why did you come here?"

"I found out that the practice was up for sale through a trade listing. Like I said previously, I wanted a mix of large and small animals and this offered it. In Northern Virginia I saw many dogs and cats that were outrageously overweight or were glorified fashion statements who weren't allowed to get their paws dirty. Now that may have been due to the clientele. It did cater to the higher income brackets. I didn't want to be in a boutique practice, I wanted a practice a bit more down to earth. Families with their well-loved pets, and large animals that aren't kept for status but had a purpose. Let's say the working animals. I was only going to find that in a rural area." Sheila tucked some hair behind her ear.

"And you ended up here."

"I did. It's close enough that if I need to get home to my parents I can."

"You're close to them?"

Sheila looked at Terri and couldn't help but notice her raised brows and her finger tapping on the table. "I am. They've been very supportive. They're my biggest fans. I realize I have been extremely fortunate."

"That's nice that you have their support, and vice versa."

They carried the dishes into the kitchen and set them aside. Sheila pulled roasted chicken breast from the oven, along with baked sweet potatoes. They carried the meal outside and enjoyed the pleasant weather.

"I noticed the book shelves in your living room have quite a selection. Who is your favorite author?" Terri asked.

"Oh, well that would depend on the genre. For horror I enjoy the master, Stephen King."

"You read horror?" Terri's eyebrows raised.

"Of course. There is nothing like a good scary book and he is superb. For crime thrillers, I like Angela Marson's Detective Kim Stone series.

"I've read a few of those. I picked the first one up while in England last summer. It was very good. I usually save those for when I am traveling."

"I would rather read than go to the movies. I like settling on the couch with a glass of wine, the fire crackling, and a good book."

"It is hard to beat. What are you currently reading?"

Sheila sipped her wine, then dabbed at her mouth with her napkin. "Umm, well I am currently reading a nonfiction book. The Gifts of Imperfection by Brené Brown." Sheila stopped talking when a huge smile crossed Terri's face. "You're familiar with her work?"

"Yes. I finished that one a few weeks ago. I've read several of her books. They're very helpful. She has some very good observations on human behavior and desires."

"She does. I hope to see her speak one day. So, what do you like to read?"

"I enjoy crime novels and legal thrillers. Of course, when I'm tired I will turn on the TV and catch up on a series. I do like Madam Secretary."

"I've never seen it."

"You might like it. It has a woman in the lead role as the Secretary of State. It's in its fourth season, but it's available online, so you could see it from the beginning."

"I've heard about it. Maybe I'll look at it."

As they carried the dishes inside after dinner, Terri looked toward the piano. "Do you play often?"

Sheila looked up from loading the dishwasher, "I'm getting back into the habit of playing. I play about thirty minutes a day. It's very relaxing."

"Would you play something?"

Sheila looked at Terri and saw the glimmer of hope in them. "Ah...I haven't played in front of anyone for some time. I'll give it a try. No throwing produce if you don't like it."

Terri laughed. "I think you're safe from that."

Sheila sat down at the piano and stretched her fingers. After a few moments she started to play a lively tune that reminded Terri of something that would be played in an old west saloon. Terri noticed a smile on Sheila's face as her fingers moved across the keyboard. *She really enjoys this. This is how she unwinds.* Terri's heart stuttered when Sheila looked up suddenly and met her eyes. Several seconds passed before she realized Sheila had stopped playing. She cleared her throat, "That sounded vaguely familiar. What was it?"

"Rose Leaf Rag by Joplin. It's played in several western movies."

"That's why it sounded vaguely familiar. Will you play something else?"

"Sure."

A few seconds later Terri laughed out loud when Sheila played Chopsticks. When Sheila continued to play Terri realized there was more to the song than the familiar opening notes. Terri clapped as Sheila finished playing. "I didn't know the song continued. Do you play everything from memory?"

"Oh, no. I mix it up. For the more complicated arrangements or pieces that I am less familiar with, I need the sheet music. I'll play one more. I think you'll recognize it." Sheila thumbed through some sheet music before placing one against the music rack. "I haven't played this for some time. It always makes me happy. It reminds me of a time when my parents and I were driving to church one spring morning and the noise of the car passing startled some lambs. They took off running. This was playing on the radio, and I remember laughing when I saw them run."

Sheila started to play and after several stanzas, she spoke, "It's called 'Morning Has Broken.' It's by Cat Stevens."

"I knew I've heard it before, but I couldn't have named it." Terri leaned against the wall listening while Sheila continued the piece. Several times their eyes met and held. Each time Terri felt warmth surge through her.

Sheila finished the tune and placed the sheet music back on the short stack of pages and lowered the fall board over the keys. "Let's have dessert. I picked up some key lime tarts from Natasha's. Would you like some coffee?"

Terri shook her head slightly. "I'll pass on the coffee. It will keep me up all night."

Sheila placed the plate of tarts on the table. "Tell me how Tripod is doing with the harness."

Terri groaned, "I don't even have it put together yet. It has a lot more pieces than I thought it would. And it only came with pictograms instructions. Why can't they actually use words for the directions?"

"If you like I can come by tomorrow and help you. Sometimes an extra set of hands is beneficial especially when putting the wheels on the axle."

"I accept. Thank you. I should get going. It's been a long day. Thank you for dinner it was delicious."

Sheila walked Terri out, they lingered by her jeep, and their eyes met, each searching for some signal. Terri's nipples hardened when

Sheila's gaze drifted to her breasts before moving upward and held on Terri's mouth for a moment, before she stepped away.

Sheila blushed and smiled. "I'm so glad you could come over."

Terri grinned, "Thanks for inviting me. I'll see you tomorrow."

As she drove away, Terri glanced in the rearview mirror and saw Sheila standing outside. *God, she was so sexy.* On the short ride back to her house, Terri thought about the day. She wasn't sure what was going on with Sheila. Several times she had felt Sheila looking at her intently—with clear sexual interest—but she didn't pursue it. Was Sheila finding herself? Was she lonely and thinking about experimenting? Was her marriage so bad that she swore off men? Or is she just shy? Whatever the cause, with the conflicting signals Sheila was sending, Terri thought she'd better tread carefully.

If Terri made a move and Sheila was not interested, would she remain quiet or would she drag Terri out of the closet? That was not something she was willing to risk. It had proven too costly for her in the past. She rubbed at her shoulder unconsciously as she continued down the road.

Chapter Seven

TERRI WATCHED AS SHEILA knelt on the floor and tightened the last of the fasteners on the harness. Watching her concentrate, Terri was aware of her own heartbeat accelerating, of a gnawing hunger low in her belly. The sexual tension continued to build, and she could no longer ignore it. Sheila looked up, their eyes met and held, energy passing between them. Terri raised her hand, gently pulling Sheila to her feet, cradled her chin in her palm and leaned forward pressing her lips to Sheila's. She held the kiss for several seconds as her tongue flicked over Sheila's lips.

Sheila's eyes opened wide as she stepped back and away from the harness. Terri stood, mortified. "I'm sorry. I thought you were interested." *Damn it*. She watched as Sheila took several more steps away, her fingers touching her lips. "Sheila, please don't go, I promise it won't happen again."

"Oh, I think it will." Before Terri could think, Sheila, with a small grin on her face, stepped forward capturing her mouth. Soft lips explored as her own lips parted, accepting Sheila's tongue before responding. The kiss, soft and sensual, grew more passionate. Terri tugged on Sheila's hair, deepening the kiss as longing raced through her, settling between her legs. Sheila's hands moved across her back and shoulders, drifted down to her waist, holding her tight. She heard her own low, throaty groan and shuddered.

Terri pulled back a little and looked at Sheila's eyes, and saw that her pupils were dilated with desire. She felt Sheila tremble as she placed soft feathery kisses and gentle licks down her neck. Sheila's skin quivered as she smoothed her hands down her sides then up under her blouse and a soft gasp broke free.

Their mouths met again, a fierce passionate kiss that Terri felt consumed by. With fire igniting inside her, she became wet, an ache pulsing in her core. Her own nipples hardened when Sheila moaned, and hands caressed along her waist. She cupped Sheila's breasts, lifting them, fondling them, and her thumbs rasped over fabric-covered nipples, causing them to pebble.

Leaning forward she nipped experimentally at Sheila's collarbone. She heard the quick gasp of surprise and soothed instantly with gentle strokes of her tongue. Her hands stroked across smooth skin and firm belly. She paused, looked at Sheila, held her gaze and slowly released the top button on her blouse. Sheila smiled in approval as Terri lowered her mouth to the exposed skin, tasting the sweetness of flesh and smelling the soft citrus scent of her soap. "You smell so good." Terri released each button and sampled the exposed flesh. Sheila's soft moans of pleasure caused Terri's heart to race. She swept the blouse back to Sheila's elbows but not off. She tickled Sheila's skin with her fingers as she moved around to release her bra and closed her teeth gently on silk-covered nipples.

Sheila's hands gripped tightly onto her hips and she arched into Terri's mouth. Sheila pulled their hips together as Terri swept her blouse and bra to the floor. She backed Sheila against the counter and felt her shudder and moan. Her own desire flared when hands tugged at her hair, directing her mouth to the exposed breasts. Terri used lips, teeth, tongue and fingers to layer sensation on Sheila's breasts until Sheila cried out and her legs shook as the orgasm ripped through her.

Slowly Terri traced her way back up until she captured Sheila's mouth in a kiss that was sensual and full of promise but not demand. She stroked a finger along Sheila's jaw and lips. With her mouth hovering barely off Sheila's she whispered, "Did that feel good?"

Sheila nodded as Terri leaned in, forehead to forehead, and wrapped her into a warm hug. As Sheila's breathing returned to normal, Terri picked up the bra and shirt and helped her put both back on, buttoning it and watching Sheila's face carefully for any regrets.

"Wait, let me—" Sheila reached for Terri's hands.

"No. Really, I'm okay. I think we need to talk about this."

Terri poured Sheila a glass of wine, grabbed a beer for herself, twisted off the cap and took a long swallow. Handing Sheila the wine, she kissed her softly. "Let's sit down."

Sheila's still-flushed cheeks brightened further. "Is something wrong? God, I've never...ah...orgasmed from breast play before."

"Really? Well, good for us. You're incredibly sensitive." Sheila's blush deepened. "Don't be embarrassed, you were beautiful. I'm glad I could give that to you." Terri took another long pull on her beer and watched as Sheila sipped her wine.

"Why did you stop me from touching you?"

"I didn't want you to have any regrets."

Sheila's eyes clouded with confusion. "Regrets? How?"

"You were married. To a man. I want you to be sure, not caught up in the heat of the moment and later regret anything."

"So, you stopped. Aren't you—"

"Aroused? You have no idea. But I want you to be sure before you try anything new."

Sheila was quiet for a moment; it was time to be more open with Terri. "I'm bisexual, Terri. It's not completely new, but I'm definitely rusty." Terri set her beer down. "My husband knew that I was bisexual but once we were dating I was only with him. I remained faithful to him, always. He did not. We were married five years. During the last year we lived apart as the divorce went through. Bastard was banging her for at least a year before I found out."

"I'm sorry."

"Don't be." Sheila sipped at her wine, hesitating briefly. "As soon as I found out I kicked him out of our house and got tested for every STD known. Fortunately, everything checked out okay." She paused, took another sip. "I haven't been with anyone since then. I haven't wanted to be. But Terri, what happened here, I would have stopped it if I didn't want what was happening." She leaned forward, lifted Terri's hand, and kissed it softly on the knuckles. "Thank you for thinking enough of me that you wanted me to be sure."

Terri picked up her beer, took a long drink. "I'll get checked. I don't have anything, but I want you to have proof."

"Terri, you don't have to."

"Yes, I do. There's a clinic in Charlotte that caters to lesbians and bisexuals. I'll go there."

"Charlotte? That's several hours away. You're not out, are you?"

"No. A few close friends know, but otherwise, it's no one's business. I would prefer to keep it that way. It's not the metropolis of Northern Virginia, things are a little more conservative here in a small town. I see the local physician when I need to, but for my sexual health I prefer the clinic in Charlotte. The larger city offers a layer of anonymity that I prefer. I have to go there tomorrow for a quick business trip. I'll stop at the clinic."

Their conversation was cut short by Sheila's cell phone ringing. She grimaced, "I have to answer this. It's the clinic." Sheila stepped out onto the porch to take the call. A few moments later she returned. "I'm sorry I need to go, there's a problem at one of the stables."

"I understand. We can talk later." Terri gave Sheila a quick peck on the cheek. "Good luck."

***

Terri emerged from the shower, toweled off quickly, finger-styled her damp hair and slid into bed. The sheets were cool and crisp against her bare skin. The cool shower had done nothing to diminish her arousal. She lay in bed, restless, trying to clear her mind, but with a heavy sigh she sat up. Tripod came into her room and stood silently watching her.

"You can't sleep either, huh girl?" Terri got up and slid into light sweatpants, flip-flops and a T-shirt, and together they went outside. The full moon lit up the ground almost as bright as daylight. They walked slowly along the wood line. The dog stopped several times, fur standing on end. Terri stopped, listening also, and heard the scratch of raccoons in the woods.

"Good girl. That's the raccoons, you should leave them alone. I wouldn't mind if you kept them out of the garbage can though."

They meandered back to the porch and sat on the steps. "I have something I want to try on you tomorrow. Sheila and I were putting it together." She smiled when Tripod's tail thumped with the mention of the name. "Yeah, she makes me happy, too." The dog lay next to Terri, its head in her lap. She gently stroked behind Tripod's ears, "Hopefully you'll try this thing, it will be easier for you to go for a walk." Tripod jumped to her feet and stood barking excitedly, tail wagging violently. "Ssh! You know 'walk', do you?" The word sent the dog into another barking frenzy as she hobbled across the porch.

"Well, we'll see how you like it tomorrow. Let's go inside." Tripod stood for a moment and whined. "Not now, in the morning." Terri watched as the dog groaned before hopping inside and went to her bed, circled three times, and lay down.

Terri went into the bedroom and opened the windows a little to let in fresh air and night sounds. Slipping out of her clothes and into bed, she recalled the afternoon—the overwhelming desire to kiss, followed by the quick panic that she had misunderstood the interest that seemed mutual, to the surge of lust that jetted through her when Sheila kissed her back. She was consumed by fire—by need so strong—that she had rushed along.

Finally, she had gained her senses enough to not go further. It hadn't been easy to stop, she wanted to feel Sheila buck and groan under her. She was surprised and thrilled when Sheila orgasmed from breast play and considered that it might have been from Sheila not having sex in over a year.

Bisexual though? That was new. Terri's prior lovers had all been lesbian. *Would Sheila's attraction to both sexes be a problem? She had remained faithful to her husband; would she be with a woman?* After several deep breaths, and with the sounds of owls calling in the woods Terri finally drifted into sleep.

***

Sheila sat on her bedroom balcony looking out at the brilliant moon and the way the trees cast shadows on her manicured lawn. Good God, she didn't know what was more embarrassing—that she had come from some passionate kissing and having her boobs played with, or the fact that she hadn't even been able to think clearly enough to touch Terri at all.

She wasn't some virginal teenager in the backseat, having her first go round. She had dated women and men, and she certainly knew her way around the bedroom. But today, holy cow, she was swept up in sensation and desire. Her orgasm had left her weak and embarrassed. Sheila sighed, Terri was right. They had needed to stop.

The conversation afterward had been revealing for both. Terri seemed relieved that she was bisexual, not just willing and horny enough to try something new. And Terri had stopped, not wanting to cause any regrets. A generous lover who looked out for her partner's well-being. That was something else Sheila could get used to feeling again. With a sigh and a promise to be more engaged the next time they were intimate, she walked back into the bedroom and fell asleep.

Chapter Eight

"COME ON, TRIPOD, STAY still." Terri stretched her arms wide before dropping them to her side. The dog once again backed away from her when she tried to put the harness on her. She called the dog back over, but Tripod lay and refused to stand. Terri sighed and rubbed her hand along on the back of her neck and leaned over the dog. "Don't you want to go for a walk?" Tripod rose, barking and prancing, head-butting Terri hard enough to knock her over, and then stood lapping at her face. With stars in her eyes and the coppery taste of blood in her mouth, Terri sat up, and ruffled the dog's neck and was surprised to see Sheila standing in the doorway with concern on her face.

"That looked like it hurt." Tripod turned and barked fiercely once before realizing it was Sheila. The bark was replaced immediately with tail thumping and whining.

"Come on in, I don't think I can stand up yet."

"Are you okay?"

"I need a minute. My head hurts and I bit my tongue. Damn she has a hard head."

Sheila knelt at Terri's side, petting the dog's head. "Tripod, you need to be more careful." She nearly laughed when the dog lay down and put a paw over its nose. "Do you want some ice?"

"No, I'll be fine." Terri started to stand up, staggered a bit, and felt Sheila grab her arm tightly, helping her rise to her feet. "Damn, she hit me hard."

"Here, come sit down." Sheila led Terri to the sofa and helped her sit. "I'm getting you some ice. Is your tongue bleeding?"

"I think it stopped."

She handed Terri the ice bag, "Put that on your head and open your mouth." Terri hesitated, and Sheila chided her. "Oh, come on, let me see." She looked in Terri's mouth. "That looks like it's going to hurt. It's not bleeding now but it's scratched. How's your head? Do you have aspirin?"

"In the medicine cabinet."

"I'll be right back." She hurried to the bathroom, returning quickly. "Here, take these. I gather she didn't want to get in the harness?" She then handed Terri two little white pills and a glass of water. Only then did she sit down.

"That's an understatement." Tripod was standing, resting her head in Terri's lap and licking at the scar on the back of her hand. "I'm not going to be able to get her in it without help."

"She just needs to get used to it. Once she realizes what it is for she'll stay still for you."

Terri voiced her obvious skepticism with a brief "Hmmph."

"You're both still getting to know each other, and you don't know what she went through before. Give her time." She tucked a lock of hair behind Terri's ear, leaned forward and kissed her softly on the lips. "There, that should make it feel all better."

Terri laughed. "Maybe if I could get a few more of those it would." Sheila leaned in and kissed her again. "Mmm, that's much better. I hope I don't need to buy a helmet for when I try to put that contraption on her."

"We can try again in a little bit. I wanted to talk to you about yesterday."

A small line appeared between Terri's eyes. "I didn't mean to rush you."

"Don't panic. I enjoyed it, obviously. I feel a little guilty, it was so one-sided."

Terri placed her fingers over Sheila's mouth silencing her. "I don't keep score. Believe me, it was pleasurable for both of us. That's what matters."

"I just feel..."

Terri pulled Sheila forward, covered her mouth with her own, and when Sheila sighed she broke the kiss. "Stop apologizing. Now, will you help me get this thing on her?"

It took several tries, but they finally got the front portion of the harness around Tripod's chest and shoulders and fastened the straps snugly. With Terri lifting Tripod off her hind leg, Sheila gently positioned the back paw into its sling.

Tripod squirmed and whimpered and tried to scooch away, but Terri held tight, talking to her softly. After checking to be sure the device was aligned correctly, Sheila opened the door. Together they coaxed the dog forward. After much encouragement she walked out of the house and across the porch, tail wagging violently. They both grabbed for her before she tried to take the chair down the steps. "I guess I better build a little ramp or I'll have to put it on her out here."

"It'll get easier. Let's take her around and see how she does on the driveway, and the wood path where it's a little rockier."

Forty minutes later they returned to the house, with a tired but happy dog. Sheila opened and closed cabinets finding what she needed to put lunch together for them, while Terri called a handyman and arranged for him to come by to see what type of ramp would be needed.

Terri finished the call and came inside.

"The sandwiches and salad look great." Terri said as they sat down to eat. "He'll be by sometime this week. I think I want the ramp next to the steps. Do you think that harness is sturdy enough that she'll be able to run? If she's healthy enough, of course."

Sheila smiled. "You sound so excited. Tripod is healthy. She's just three-legged. She can run with the harness, it's built to be sturdy. There's actually a video online of a group of dogs playing fetch while wearing them."

"That's good to know." Terri heard Sheila's phone ring. "You should get that, it might be important."

Terri cleared the dishes as Sheila took her call. She looked over when she heard Sheila's gentle sigh. "I'll be there in ten minutes." She disconnected the call. "I'm sorry, I have to go."

"I understand." Terri was surprised when Sheila captured her mouth in a hot possessive kiss that left her head spinning.

"Have a good evening." Terri stood motionless, her heart pounding. She was stunned by the hunger in the kiss. After staring into space a few minutes, she peered at the sleeping dog and went into her office to start working.

Chapter Nine

SHEILA PRESSED HER HAND against her chest and felt her racing heart. She looked at her car assessing the damage. Both tires on the right were blown, and the muffler dragging. *I should have hit the deer. It probably would have cost less.* It had run in front of her, she overcorrected and ended up in a ditch. She hadn't seen a car in fifteen minutes. *Where the hell is everyone?* The service had said the tow truck would be along shortly. She had called Terri at home and on her cell and left messages. Several minutes had passed and her heart was finally slowing down. Her phone pinged. Glancing at the message she smiled. Terri would be there in about ten minutes. She went through her car and pulled out the files she had, her medical bag, and her purse.

Leaning on the hood of her car, she heard the rumble of a motorcycle. A blue and chrome bike came into view and slowed. Dressed in leather, a shiny black helmet, and sturdy boots, the driver offered a small wave, and drove past. "Figures," she muttered. She stiffened and looked over her shoulder and watched as the driver turned the bike back toward her. The dark visor obscured the driver's face. Sheila became suddenly aware that she was quite isolated. She reached into her purse for her pepper spray and remembered she had stopped carrying it now that she didn't live in the city. The driver stopped the bike and swung off. Sheila looked desperately around for any type of weapon that she could use to defend herself if necessary, she held back the urge to run and reached inside her car for the keys. She could jab with them if needed. Her apprehension grew when the rider reached into a storage bin and pulled something out. With her heart hammering, Sheila watched as the rider turned toward her. The rider stopped, reached up and removed the helmet. Sheila shuddered and blew out a breath as Terri smiled at her.

"Are you okay? You look pretty shaken up." Terri closed the distance between them and took Sheila gently by the arms. "Are you hurt? Did you hit your head?"

"No. Thank God it's you. I didn't know you had a motorcycle."

"I've had it for a couple of years. Are you sure you're okay?"

"I thought...I was afraid of...when you turned around and drove back, I didn't know it was you. I suddenly realized how alone I was."

"I didn't mean to scare you." Terri brushed some of Sheila's hair back behind her ear. "I'm sorry, I should have raised my visor or told you I was on the bike."

Sheila stood, momentarily shocked with the quick sizzle that went through her at Terri's touch. Before she could respond, the sound of a truck coming down the road reached them. Together, they watched as the tow truck pulled up. The driver stopped, looked at Sheila, then at Terri, and smiled broadly. "Hey, Terri! I see you got the bike out today. It's a beautiful day for it."

"Hey, Jackson. Good to see you." She walked over to the tow truck and shook the driver's hand. "How's business?"

"Been good." He stepped out of the truck and glanced over at Sheila's car. "It's getting better. It's tourist season, you know. Looking at all our pretty mountains they drive right off the road."

Sheila started to protest, but Terri cut her off. "This is Dr. McDevitt. She took over for Dr. James."

"Is that so? I heard she was quite a looker. For a woman." Jackson and Terri laughed as she punched him gently on the shoulder. Sheila felt heat rise to her cheeks but was confused at the statement. "Move your ride, Terri, so I can get this rig in there."

"Sure thing." Terri moved the bike and leaned on it while Sheila and Jackson completed the necessary paperwork. He put the spare on the rear axle then hooked the car up to the tow truck.

Before he pulled off, he came back, and handed Sheila her copy of the paperwork. "Hey, Doc, you want to ride on the back of that thing or up here with me?" He was well over six feet, two hundred-fifty pounds, and had a scruffy beard. Before she could politely decline, Terri handed her a helmet.

"She's going with me, Jackson." She kissed him quickly on the cheek. "It's been a while. Give me a call and we'll get a beer."

Sheila watched the exchange with interest. Had Terri had a relationship with this giant of a man?

They watched as he drove off. "Have you ever been on a bike before?" Terri asked.

"No."

Terri grinned, took the helmet from Sheila's hands and put it on her head. "Well, get ready because there is nothing like it." She fastened the chinstrap and stroked a finger across Sheila's cheek. "Hold on tight, lean into the turns. When we turn right look over my right shoulder, if we're turning left look over the left." Terri took Sheila's purse and medical bag, putting them in a storage bin and placed the files in the other.

"After you get on, put your feet on those pegs." Terri put on her own helmet, pushed both their visors down and swung onto the bike. She started it, reached out her hand to steady Sheila as she climbed on. "Ready?"

Sheila whispered, "Yes."

Terri pulled out onto the road and Sheila hesitated before placing her hands on Terri's hips. No extra padding there. The bike started to move and with a quick intake of breath, her fingers flexed, digging in for a few seconds before relaxing slightly. It didn't take long for Sheila to wrap her arms further around Terri's waist. As they picked up speed, the noise of the engine, the road, and the wind blended into a soft, steady whoosh. Terri revved the engine and the bike immediately responded, and Sheila tightened her grip.

The bike rolled into a turn, Sheila tensed, and Terri shouted, "Relax, move with the bike, don't fight it."

Sheila rolled her neck and shoulders and took several deep breaths. After a few more seconds she began looking around and enjoyed the view. She realized she was seeing more now than during any other trip. Of course, that was partly because she could look around, as she wasn't busy driving. But that wasn't it entirely. She felt surrounded by nature, as if she was taking part in it. The wind and the sun both beating on her were freeing. The throb of the bike in her ears and—good Lord—between her legs, stimulating. No wonder people liked to ride these things.

They came to an intersection and Terri slowed the bike, bringing it to a stop. While they waited for the traffic to clear, she could smell the leather of Terri's jacket, the subtle smell of her soap, and a faint spicy perfume. "Are you in a rush?"

"No, this is fun."

"Do you want to keep going?"

"Could we? This is...invigorating."

"Great." Terri swung the bike onto another road. They started up the mountains, twisting and winding along the road as they moved in and out of shadows. Flowers bloomed on the trees around them, their fragrance on the wind.

Sheila wanted to throw her arms up and shout with the exhilaration she was feeling but did not dare to let go. Thirty minutes later they drove into a town, and Terri pulled the bike to the side of the main street and turned it off.

"Do you think you can get off? Just swing your leg over."

Sheila did as she was told. She wobbled on her feet for a second, but Terri grabbed her arm.

"Hold on." Terri lowered the stand, dismounted and pulled off her helmet. "Are you okay?"

"I lost my balance for a second. I'm good now." Sheila looked around. "Where are we?"

"Near Robbinsville. There's a great ice cream shop here. Would you like some?"

"Yes, would love some." Terri stood smiling at her. "Which way?"

"It's down the street a bit." Terri gestured to the right then at her head. "You might want to take off the helmet though."

"Oh! I forgot." Before she could reach for it, Terri unhooked the chinstrap and her hand lingered on Sheila's chin. The warmth from Terri's hand was comforting and Sheila pressed into it. Their eyes met and held. Sheila's tongue darted out to moisten her lips, and Terri started to lean in but stopped when a horn sounded somewhere close by. They both jumped, and with the moment passed Sheila slipped the helmet from her head then fluffed her hair. "Where do we put..."

Terri took the helmet from her and strapped both helmets to the seat. "The shop is this way."

As they walked to their destination, Sheila asked, "How do you know Jackson?"

"Well, he did some work on my Jeep when I first got here. He's one of two tow truck drivers nearby."

"He seems nice. He's a big guy. Pretty intimidating."

"Yeah, he is pretty big. Wouldn't hurt a flea though."

"You seem pretty close."

Terri looked over at her. "I guess so. As close as he is to any woman. Or vice versa." Sheila looked confused. "Jackson is gay. A couple years ago some guys in one of the other towns started to pick on him. He stood there and took it. He was afraid if he started fighting, he would hurt them. A couple of nights later they came over to our neck of the woods and tried to get something stirred up. I helped him out by being his date that night. It quieted down the speculation for both of us." They reached the shop with a light green and white awning, which provided shade for several tables. They ordered their ice cream and returned outdoors. "They make their own ice cream here. It's a little more expensive, but worth it."

Terri flicked her tongue delicately over the peach ice cream cone. Sheila watched, mesmerized, and couldn't help but remember what that tongue had felt like on her breasts. She wondered what that tongue would feel like elsewhere.

"How did you get in the ditch?" Flick, flick.

"A deer ran out in front, then a fawn. I swerved, went too far and I couldn't get off the shoulder of the road. Then the tires blew." Flick, flick. She pressed a hand to her stomach to calm the butterflies as her cheeks warmed.

"Why were you out that way?" Flick, flick. Sheila was silent. "Sheila?"

She looked up to see Terri's amused smile. "What? Sorry I, um, thought of something. I forgot." A long sweep of tongue around the cone. "What did you ask?" *Good God.*

"Where were you heading to?"

"I was coming back to town from Red Oak stables. They had a colt born last night. It was a difficult delivery for the mare, so I was checking on them."

"Red Oak? Their road is horrible. You're lucky you didn't break down out there. You could do some serious damage to your car. You need a truck."

"A truck?"

"Yes. If you're going to be going out to farms and stables, you'll need a bigger vehicle with better ground clearance. Plus, you won't look like a tourist." Flick, flick. Sheila squirmed. "Put the name of your clinic on the side, get some more visibility."

"Hmmm, I'll think about it." Heat spread across her neck, and her nipples tightened. *God, I want her.* She hurriedly ate her chocolate ice cream, hoping for a brain freeze to distract her.

Terri finished her ice cream, wiped her hands on the napkin and threw it away. "There are a couple of places nearby that could give you a good deal. You might even be able to get a used one for a good price. It wouldn't be as expensive, and you wouldn't be so upset when it gets dinged around some."

"I'll look into it." Sheila finished her cone and tossed the napkin away.

"Ready to go?"

Sheila looked into Terri's deep brown eyes and was suddenly speechless from the intensity of the gaze. She nodded her head, unable to speak out loud. They walked back to the motorcycle with Terri pointing out a few of the merchants. They got to the bike, put on their helmets, and Terri climbed on. The bike rumbled to life, as Sheila fastened her chinstrap. Sheila hesitated before climbing on.

"What's wrong?"

"It's...nothing." *Between the bike vibration and that look, I'm so aroused I could slide off the seat.* Finally, she swung her leg over and sat down. "I'm ready." She smirked when Terri's abdomen quivered as she wrapped her arms around her waist. *Thank God, it's not just me.*

***

Terri accelerated smoothly. She was able to suppress her groan but not the clenching in her abdomen as Sheila tightened her grip. The air was starting to chill as the sun drifted lower in the sky, casting long shadows across the road. She felt Sheila shiver. "Move close to me to stay warm. Let me know if you get too cold." A moment later she felt Sheila lean into her and hug her tighter. Over the next twenty minutes Sheila would occasionally squirm, and her legs would press tighter against Terri's hips. A deep ache settled in Terri's core. Thirty minutes later she made the turn onto the road up to her cabin.

"Hold on tight, it gets bumpy." Terri drove the bike confidently up the steep bumpy road. Finally, it leveled off and she turned into her driveway. Stopping the bike, she turned it off and waited while Sheila got off and removed her helmet. She then swung off, and quickly removed her own. "Are you warm enough?"

"Yes. Now that the wind stopped. I'm fine."

"Good." Terri pulled Sheila toward her in a fierce, passionate kiss that had both breathless in seconds. Desire raced through her body and her heart pounded. She tightened her arms around Sheila's waist and her body nearly vibrated with the intensity of the kiss. Sheila's hands grasped at the stiff leather of Terri's clothes. Terri tugged at Sheila's shirt freeing it from her jeans. The kiss broke, and Sheila nearly staggered as Terri took her hand and pulled her to the porch. She backed Sheila up against the doorframe and held her hands above her head as their mouths met again, the intensity of the kiss sending arrows of heat to her core.

Tripod woofed softly from inside, breaking the spell. Terri sighed in frustration, unlocked the door and held it open for Sheila. Sheila hesitated before walking in and Terri thought she would explode. They stood looking at each other, the pulse in Sheila's neck visible, her cheeks flushed, and her pupils wide. Sheila stroked her hand along Terri's cheek as she walked inside. Tripod forced her way between them and nudged Terri toward the door.

"I'll take her out. Why don't you pour us some wine? I'll be back in a few minutes." Terri paced as the dog slowly circled the yard. She tried to slow her breathing and shivered, thinking of Sheila inside waiting. Tripod dropped a ball at Terri's feet. *Oh God, not now.* Tripod nuzzled her hand so she tossed the ball and waited as Tripod hobbled back with it. She looked at the bike and laughed out loud. They should be called vibracycles. Tripod started to roll on the grass as she started the bike, moving it into the large shed. She retrieved Sheila's papers and bags from the storage bins and locked the door to the shed. Slowly they made their way back to the house.

***

Terri came back inside and was surprised to not see Sheila. A split second later the sound of the shower running made her smile. She placed Sheila's belongings on an end table and hung her leather jacket up. Picking up a glass of wine she sipped at it and smiling to herself, she scooped food into a bowl for Tripod. There was no need to rush, it was time to explore, have fun and savor what should be a very enjoyable evening. While the dog ate, she sipped at her wine and arranged some cheese, crackers and fruit on a small plate. She moved the food and wine over to the coffee table and put on some mellow jazz. She nibbled at the snack, and when Sheila emerged wrapped in her robe, she nearly groaned. Terri handed Sheila a glass of wine.

"I didn't think you would mind, I had to shower. I noticed that my clothes were filthy and then I remembered what I had been doing out on the farm."

"I understand. Here, come sit down, and enjoy some wine and cheese."

They sat on the leather couch and sipped wine while talking. Terri tried not to repeatedly glance at Sheila's legs. She leaned forward and ran a finger across Sheila's lips, smiling as they quivered beneath her touch. She lowered her mouth to Sheila's, gently kissing her before swiping her tongue along the seam of her lips, asking for entry. Sheila's arms were firm and warm as they wrapped around Terri's shoulders, and her throat vibrated with a soft moan.

Terri deepened the kiss, her tongue dancing with Sheila's as their mouths explored each other's and passion turned to a slow simmer. Terri moved her hand gently along the side of Sheila's jaw and cupped her chin. "I need a few minutes."

Terri showered quickly and stood momentarily in front of her closet. Her robe was presently occupied, although she hoped not for very long. She slipped into some midnight-blue silk lounging pants and matching top, finger-brushing her short hair as she went back out to the living room.

***

Sheila leaned back, nearly groaning in frustration when Terri walked to the bathroom. Please don't let her take a long shower. She nibbled at a cracker then refilled their wine. *Patience. Anticipation is exciting, seduction is part of this.* She felt her own arousal, and her breasts were tingling. She was aware her desire had been ramping up since she snuggled up to Terri on the back of that oversized vibrator. She suddenly became aware of Terri standing in the entryway, watching her.

Sheila stood and walked slowly over to her. She brushed a kiss over Terri's mouth before nibbling her ear and whispering, "I want you. Let's go to bed."

Their bodies collided, mouths fused. Sheila became vaguely aware of Terri guiding her to the bedroom. She shivered with excitement as Terri swept the robe open. Smooth, firm hands stroked across her breasts, gliding across her instantly-hardening nipples. Terri's tongue left a damp trail down her neck and across her chest before flicking playfully at her nipples, capturing first one then the other in a quick intense suck.

Sheila inhaled sharply, her hands tightening in Terri's hair, and arching into her mouth. She groaned as soothing strokes of tongue swept across her breasts and soft hands drifted down her torso. Their eyes met, and Sheila trembled when she saw the desire evident in Terri's eyes. She shivered as her legs were caressed and sat back when Terri nudged her onto the bed. Strong, firm fingers massaged her legs, and slid slowly across her abdomen as Terri stood up.

She watched breathlessly as Terri raised her shirt over her head

and pulled the silky pants off. Sheila was stunned—nearly speechless—
by Terri's physique. She had thought Terri slender but that was not
accurate. The woman who stood before her was nearly a model of
feminine athleticism. Firm, smooth muscles, a taut flat stomach, a
subtle flair of hip, and long, strong legs. A pale, thin line ran across the
middle of one thigh, but was quickly forgotten as Terri moved onto the
bed with her and guided her up into the center of the bed before
kneeling astride her and pressing soft, delicate kisses on her mouth and
jaw. Sheila shivered with anticipation as Terri lowered herself onto her
body, skin to skin, breast to breast, their bodies touching intimately.

Her heartbeat accelerated as she pulled Terri down to her and
kissed her urgently. Passion ignited and their kisses became deeper. She
felt Terri lift from her slightly and slid down to capture a nipple, teasing
it with her tongue and lips. She groaned "harder," heard Terri's small
chuckle, and looked to see Terri smiling wickedly at her before capturing
her other breast with her mouth and teasing it the same way.

Grabbing Terri's head, she forced it back to her breast. She writhed
against her, grinding her mound against Terri's tensed thigh. Firm hands
kneaded her breasts, lifting and squeezing, thumbs rasping once more
across her hardened nipples. Terri slid down further, her hands teasing,
stroking lightly across her torso, as a warm moist line of kisses followed.
Sheila moaned and shuddered as her arousal increased, her sex wet and
aching.

In agony, she moved her hips in invitation as her hands pushed
gently on Terri's shoulders. Moist flicks of tongue were followed by
warming breath, and a light trace of fingernails across her stomach.

Terri was obviously in no rush. But Sheila was desperate for Terri to
move lower, the fluttery movement of fingers stroking lightly across her
lower abdomen left her quivering. She felt Terri use her thigh to nudge
her legs apart as she slid her hands down her inner thigh, before
surprising her with a slight drag of fingernails back up to her sex.

She spread her legs further and arched up, offering herself, and felt
the softest stroke of fingers across her outer lips, a gentle squeeze as
they were pressed together, and finally lifted apart. Moist kisses along
the inner thighs had her panting as desperation grew. Fingers gently
slipped through her tuft of hair. Warm moist breath blew delicately
across her and was followed instantly by the smooth soft stroke of
tongue up her slit.

She groaned in pleasure as the action was repeated and gasped
when Terri circled her clit before sucking it gently. Light, playful strokes

of fingers, slick with her own wetness, teased her. The deep ache low in her pelvis intensified, her pussy drenched with anticipation. Her hands hurt from twisting in the sheets, she moved them to her own breasts and caressed them.

Her legs tightened, squeezing on Terri's shoulders as wetness ran from her and was laved away. She lifted her hips and was pressed back down to the bed. Her hands grasped for Terri's head to direct pressure and she moaned in desperation as the strokes she received softened. A firm stroke of finger along her clit and a barely-touched flick of tongue and she knew she would beg.

"Please." Sheila was on fire, the ache now through her burning chest. Her core pulsed and tightened, a bowstring ready to erupt. "Please." A sensual suck on her clit was paired with vigorous strokes, and she erupted in a white-hot burst of light and tension, screaming in release.

She lay shaking as Terri moved up her body, pinning one of her legs, and spreading her, fingers entering her drenched, quivering pussy. Smooth rhythmic stroking quickly had her building again, tension rising as Terri used her mouth exquisitely on her swollen breasts, alternating soft sucking with nibbles and strokes. Fingers fluttered across sensitive tissue inside her vagina. She panted and gasped as tension built to an unfamiliar intensity. Animal passion flamed as rational thought left. Her muscles strained as she pulled Terri up her body and set her teeth on her collarbone before capturing Terri's mouth in a hot, urgent kiss.

Skilled fingers continued to thrust in her. On the verge of cresting again, her gaze locked on Terri's and she saw the dark excitement in them. With the breath in her lungs backing up, her walls spasmed and clutched, and the world broke apart in a violent release. She screamed, "Terri!"

Sheila lay on her back, soaked in sweat, her legs shuddering with aftershocks. Terri nuzzled at her neck and suckled on her earlobe. Sheila turned to face her and saw the desperate need in Terri's eyes.

"Ooh. Terri, let me," She pushed Terri onto her back. Her mouth quickly found Terri's firm, small breasts, her tongue encircled her nipples, and she experimentally dragged her teeth across the peak.

Terri gasped and arched into her mouth, her hips thrusting against Sheila. She quickly moved her hand lower, finding Terri drenched. She cupped her sex, pressing the heel of her hand firmly on Terri's mound, and teased at her hair. She slid two fingers down her wet folds.

Terri's thrusting grew more urgent, and Sheila entered her with one finger. She felt the incredible tightness of her pussy and stroked the length of her walls. After stroking several times, she found her G-spot and flicked her finger across it as Terri groaned and arched. She marveled at Terri's strength when she dug her heels into the bed, lifting them both momentarily.

Sheila stroked rhythmically, added another finger, and gently massaged Terri's clit. Terri shuddered and quaked under her while she continued to nuzzle at Terri's breasts. Soon they were in rhythm, Terri's hips rising to meet the thrusts of her fingers. As Terri's breathing grew ragged, she moved up and kissed her, capturing her cry of release.

They lay entangled for several long minutes, lost in their own thoughts while they recovered. Sheila rolled over onto her side, leaning on an elbow and looking at Terri. Her lean, muscular body was still flushed with their passion. Her eyes lingered on her breasts. She felt her desire rise again, stroked her finger along Terri's firm, flat abdomen, and across the gentle swoop of breast. She looked up and saw Terri's hungry gaze. With a delicate shudder of anticipation, she realized it was going to be a long night.

***

Sheila lay in bed, somewhere between dreaming and wakefulness, and gradually became aware of the warm body lying behind her. She smiled, remembering, and pushed back into that warmth. Terri's arm came around her and settled, dead weight across her. She listened to Terri's breathing slow, steady, and comforting. Feeling the press of Terri's breasts against her back, she sighed. She couldn't remember the last time she'd awakened feeling the warm arms of a lover around her. Couldn't remember the last time she had been so thoroughly pleasured.

She attempted to roll over, felt Terri give, shift and roll. Sheila turned over, spooning lightly. She stroked her hands along Terri's shoulder, down across her back and felt the raised, jagged flesh. She remembered feeling it last night, across several areas, and now she lowered the blanket. Several thin stripes crossed her back, whiter than the surrounding flesh. And four—no, five—unusual rectangular scars of raised thickened skin, were on her shoulders and back. Looking further, stroking further, she felt another. She looked and grimaced at two additional jagged rectangles, one at the top of her right leg, another on her ass. She propped herself on an elbow, reached out and traced one of the scars on her shoulder, leaning forward and kissing it softly. Terri jolted awake, sprang from the bed and stumbled, nearly losing her balance.

"What are you doing?" she croaked, her voice gravelly with sleep.

"I was kissing you. How did you get those scars?"

Terri reached into her dresser, yanked out a support tank and pulled it on, grabbed a T-shirt and added that. "I fell on something. Cut the skin a little."

Sheila raised her eyebrows and sat up in bed. "A little?"

Terri nearly flew across the room, yanked a pair of panties on, and practically jumped into her jeans. "Yeah. Well I must have been drunk or something."

Sheila hurried over to Terri, grabbed her hand. "Come on, seriously. What happened?"

"I don't want to talk about it."

Sheila grew concerned and held tight when Terri tried to pull her hand away. "Terri", she said softly. "Who did that to you? Why?"

"It doesn't matter who did it. It won't happen again." Terri pulled her hand free and jammed them into her underarms.

"Terri, I can't force you to tell me, but I hope that you know that you can trust me."

Terri's eyes filled with tears. "It doesn't matter. It won't undo it. Don't pity me. I don't want your pity." Terri paced around the room her hands pulling at her hair until it stood up in spiky tufts.

Sheila watched helplessly as Terri's normal demeanor crumpled under duress. *She looks like she's going to climb out the window any moment to escape. That's it—escape—that's why she left New York.*

"Your family did this?" Her heart tripped in her chest. *Who could hit so hard, so many times to leave such vicious wounds?* "Your father did this? You said he was a tyrant. Strict. Is that why you're not close to your family? He beat you?"

Terri looked a shadow of herself, defeated. "He beat us all. But I was his favorite."

Sheila tried to hold back a shudder. "What are the scars from?"

"He liked the belt, but anything handy would do."

"What are the rectangles?"

"Ever see a belt buckle? It didn't matter what end he used or where. He swung and hit until he was tired."

"Why?"

Terri waved her arms around. "Why? Because he was a sadistic bastard! Get a B on a test. Bam! Get home late. Bam!" Terri got more and more agitated and started to shout. "Drop something on the floor? Bam! Be a lesbian? Bam! Bam! Add a few kicks while you're down crawling to get away. He did it because he could."

"Your mother?"

"Preferred her hands!"

"Oh Jesus, Terri! I'm so sorry." Sheila moved to hug her lover but stopped when Terri jerked backward, her arms wrapped tight across her chest.

Terri swiped at the tears streaming down her face. "I don't want your pity."

"It's sympathy, and that's too bad. You'll have it anyway." Sheila walked over and gently wrapped her arms around Terri, held tighter when Terri tried to pull free, and then held on as Terri shifted, clung to her and let her tears finally break free.

As the tears and the shudders stopped, Sheila lowered Terri onto the bed, and sat with her waiting for the emotional storm to pass. Terri leaned forward and placed her head in her hands, elbows on her knees.

"I'm sorry for what your parents did to you, Terri. I wish I could make it go away. I wish I could make you not hurt. I know you well enough to know you need some time to yourself now, but I'm only going to the kitchen. I'll get some coffee going." Sheila dropped to her knees in front of Terri, lifted her chin, and stroked her thumbs across her tear-stained cheeks. "You deserved to be loved and treated right." She leaned forward, kissed Terri on the top of the head, much as her own mother had done to her. "Come on out when you're ready."

Sheila closed the bedroom door and wiped her eyes. She took several steps before she started to shake. She pressed her hand to her aching stomach and realized she was still naked. *Oh God, I need clothes. I can't go back in there right now.* She looked in the dryer and found a pair of Terri's sweatpants and a T-shirt. Slipping the shirt on she shuddered, and she nearly fell tugging on the sweatpants. She stepped around Tripod and almost ran through the house trying to get outside before she started to cry. She made it to the porch before a muffled cry escaped and she sat down on the steps and cried.

Chapter Ten

A SHORT WHILE LATER Sheila went back inside and washed her face. She stood looking at her hands for several seconds before taking a deep breath and letting it out slowly. She found Tripod lying in front of the bathroom door. The dog lifted her head as Sheila approached but otherwise did not move. "Come on, Tripod, let's go out." The dog stayed. "Tripod, come on. Go outside." Tripod lowered her head, pulled her ears back and sniffed at the opening under the door. "You know she's hurting, don't you, girl? Okay, you stay here. I'll go get some breakfast started."

In the kitchen Sheila started coffee and cut up some fruit. Rummaging in the refrigerator, she pulled out a couple of eggs and milk. She found bread, vanilla, and nutmeg. She was still looking through the cabinets when Terri came in.

"What are you looking for?"

"Ayyahh." Sheila turned with her hand on her chest. "Damn, you scared me. I was looking for cinnamon for French toast."

Terri stepped over, reached into the cabinet and immediately found the cinnamon, handed it to Sheila, and reached for coffee mugs.

Sheila didn't like the flat expression on Terri's face. "Are you okay?"

"Yes. There's a small griddle in the drawer under the oven." Terri poured coffee, added a splash of milk to one, and handed it to Sheila. Taking her own, Terri blew on it before taking a small sip. She pulled butter out of the fridge and cranberry juice. "Do you want me to cook?"

"No, I was hoping we could talk. About you. About what you told me."

"Why? It doesn't help, and it doesn't make it so it didn't happen." Terri shrugged her shoulders, her voice flat, almost emotionless.

Sheila placed her hand on Terri's forearm. "Terri, I want to know you better. To know what makes you tick. So, I can understand why sometimes you clam up or seem tense. I don't want to hurt you, but I need to know more so I don't inadvertently do that."

"Just be honest with me, and you won't hurt me." Tripod nudged at her hand. She walked over and opened the door to let the dog out.

"You think it's that simple? I have to be honest with you, but you get to hide things?"

"That's not what I meant." Terri sighed heavily and sat down leaning her arms on the table. She held the coffee mug in both hands, warming them. "Are you sure you want to hear this?"

"No, I'm not sure. But I want to know who you are, Terri. You're more than a photographer. You've come from somewhere, you've said enough that I know your life has not been easy. But here we are, together, and I want to know more."

Terri sat for a few moments sipping her coffee quietly. "I grew up in Western New York. My parents were perfectionists. If it wasn't straight A's, you weren't trying hard enough. If your team lost and you dropped the ball or struck out or whatever, you didn't practice enough and were embarrassing them. Absolute perfection and obedience. There was verbal and physical abuse. I knew early on that things were different in my home compared to my friends. My parents would question me as to what I talked about when I was at friends' houses or even at birthday parties. If I was ever allowed to go. Even when I was young."

Sheila sat at the table across from Terri silently encouraging her to continue. "When I was fourteen, I got a job working a few hours a week at a Chinese grocery store, sweeping and stocking shelves. At first Mr. Chen wouldn't hire me because I was too young. Then one day when I came by and asked again, his wife told him to hire me. It was four hours during the week and another four on Saturdays. I found out later she had seen bruises on my arms and suspected something was wrong. They helped me with homework I didn't understand, tutored me. I kept my grades up. I worked more hours after I turned sixteen. I worked for him until I finished high school. He moved me to a different store, across town, after I left home, so my parents couldn't find me. It was closer to the friends I stayed with until I graduated."

"You left home in high school?"

"My senior year. One night I went home after work. I was two steps inside the door when I was body slammed to the floor. I knew it was my dad when I was still flying through the air. As soon as I hit the floor, he was hitting me with the belt. Screaming at me for being a lesbian, kicking me. My mother stood and watched and told him to beat it out of me. Somehow, I don't know how, I managed to get away, to get outside.

"I had left my coat in the car and had the sense to get it. I wandered around that night and ended up down at an encampment of homeless people under a bridge with a fire going to stay warm. I went to school the next day, showered in the locker room. I found an old sweatshirt in lost and found to cover up my torn shirt. I slept the next night with the homeless people again. The third day, when school was over, it was pouring rain. It was mid-March, and cold. I wasn't feeling well. I hid in the school, got into the nurse's office to get stuff to clean up the cuts. When the janitors cleaned the classrooms, I stayed out of sight. I got in the equipment room, got a hold of some school sweats, and wore those while my clothes laundered. I took shirts or sweaters, whatever I needed from the lost and found bins.

"I did that for about a week until I got caught one evening stealing food when the home economics teacher came into her classroom and caught me cooking. I had forgotten that there was an evening meeting for the teachers. My art teacher had the room next door. She heard the teacher hollering and came in to see what was going on. To make a long story short the vice principal came down. My art teacher, Laurie, was talking to me, asking me why I was doing it when I got dizzy. I fell, and she tried to catch me. I screamed because when she caught me the cuts had split open. Most of them were infected. That's why they didn't heal well, and I have the scars. I told them what had happened. They helped me. All of them. Anyhow, I didn't get suspended, and I ended up living for the rest of the school year with Laurie and her boyfriend, who was also a teacher. About two months later I started coming south."

"Terri, why didn't they report what happened to the authorities?"

"I begged them not to. And I do mean I begged. There would have been an investigation, but until it was over, there would have been a chance that I could have been sent back. I was afraid they would kill me. I'm still not convinced they wouldn't have. The home ec teacher started teaching me how to cook. Her boyfriend, a phys ed teacher, taught me how to fight, so I would be able to protect myself. I kept working with Mr. Chen. He had always paid me fairly, but after graduation they gave me a thousand dollars. He said they had been putting money aside for me, because they wanted me to have a chance. The Chens came to my graduation. A few of my teachers and the Chens gave me my first camera, as a graduation gift. I had seen it at a pawn shop and was saving money for it. It was a dream I wasn't likely to achieve, but it was something to aim for. Anyhow, I knew I couldn't stay with my teachers forever, and after I took care of a few things, I thanked everyone, and I left."

"Did your parents ever look for you?"

"Why would they have?"

Sheila stared, dumbfounded. "You were their child."

"No, I was their punching bag." Terri finished her coffee, got up quickly, and wiping a tear from her eye, walked away. Sheila followed her into the kitchen. Placed her hands on Terri's shoulders turning her slowly and hugged her tight. She swallowed hard when Terri shuddered and blew out a jagged breath. After a few moments Terri pulled back, her voice barely above a whisper. "I've never told that to anyone before." She was silent for a moment before she turned back toward the counter and started to crack the eggs in a bowl and asked, "French toast, huh? Do you like a lot of nutmeg?"

Before she could do anything else, Sheila nudged her aside. She lifted Terri's hand to her lips and kissed the scar there. "I was cooking breakfast. You can set the table. Terri? Thank you for telling me."

Chapter Eleven

SHEILA WAS EXHAUSTED. THE last three days had been busy and intense. She welcomed the business, but she was dead tired. Several animals had been hit by cars and needed surgery while some never made it that far. A run of feline influenza had cat owners bringing their pets in. The staff had been great, pitching in and working extra hours. The additional business brought a sigh of relief as well as fatigue. The ever-present concern that she would have to lay off staff or cut their hours was less a worry for at least a few days.

Sheila checked her personal bank account and saw that Peter had made a deposit. She shouted out loud, "Son of a bitch! You sent half the money. Damn it! Fine, you want to play dirty pool. Two can play that game."

She spent the next twenty minutes discussing the partial alimony payment with her lawyer. Looking at her watch, she noticed it was five-thirty. The staff had already left. She would make one last check on the animals, and then she would head home.

Terri should be back later that evening. With a little luck she would spend the night. They had been staying together one or two nights a week. Sheila smiled. She had enjoyed more sex in the last month then she had in the last two years that she was married. Not just more, but better. Terri was an energetic and imaginative lover. Sheila was surprised at how difficult it was to sleep without Terri beside her. She had never been one to snuggle, but she found herself reaching for her lover during the night and waking when her arms were empty. She hadn't had a good night's sleep since Terri left.

***

Terri started downloading files from her camera, unloaded her suitcase, and started laundry. Rummaging through the kitchen, she made a quick grocery list and planned a few meals for the days ahead.

Going back upstairs, she checked her equipment, cleaning it when necessary, and set the batteries on their chargers. Looking at the time, she considered for a moment before deciding to combine her run with the trip to the clinic to get Tripod.

She had missed Sheila, perhaps more than she wanted to admit to herself. And to be honest, that scared her. Everything had progressed very quickly. She had disclosed parts of her life to Sheila that she had told no one previously. Her openness with Sheila concerned her at times, left her feeling vulnerable. Restless from her long drive and low energy chores, she changed into running gear, stretched, and headed out.

Terri got to the clinic forty minutes later and noticed the silver-gray pickup truck in the parking lot with the clinic's name and number on it. No BMW around. Terri smiled. *So, Sheila got the pickup, and hadn't even said anything about it.* She quietly opened the clinic door, saw no one was around, and walked into Sheila's office. She stood for a moment, watching Sheila work at the computer, and felt a twinge deep in her gut. She knew the moment Sheila sensed her presence.

Sheila looked up, surprised and jumped to her feet moving toward Terri. "You're back!"

Terri held up her hands stopping her. "I'm pretty sweaty. I ran over. I don't want to get you all icky." She leaned in and kissed Sheila. "You've been busy."

"We have been. It's been crazy the last few days. How was your trip?"

"Good. I'll have editing to do later, but for now I'm caught up. You got a truck."

"Yes. It's surprisingly comfortable to drive. I like it."

"Good, you can take me for a ride in it later. I'm going to be too tired to run all the way back home." Terri paused and watched as Sheila looked away, trying to hide a smirk. "What's wrong? You're blushing."

"No, I'm not." Her hands went to her cheeks concealing them.

Terri stepped closer. "What naughty thought were you thinking?"

Sheila stuttered. "You...you said I should take you for a ride. I ..."

She stopped talking as Terri leaned in close and whispered, "I think you missed me. I missed you a lot. I think you want me to take you. Right here. Right now."

"I...oh God!" Terri watched as Sheila ran out to the entrance, locked it, set the alarm, and then ran back into the office. "You're so damn sexy, all hot and sweaty."

"Am I? I wonder how sexy you're going to look when you're the same way." She fisted her hand in Sheila's hair, tugged her head back and took quick possession of her mouth. Her other hand worked quickly to open Sheila's pants. She slipped her hand under Sheila's panties and against her sex. Her fingers slid lower. "Oh, baby, you're so wet." Terri slipped two fingers inside, stroked her walls, and started moving slow and deep. She nipped at Sheila's ear. "You are so wet for me. Did you miss me?"

"Yes." Sheila panted.

"Is this what you want?"

"Yes."

Terri nipped again on her earlobe, pinched a nipple, and felt it harden. "Tell me what you want." She stroked deeper, her thumb circling but not touching her engorged clit. Sheila groaned and started to rhythmically thrust her hips in time with Terri's skilled stroking. She clutched at Terri's arms when the stroking stopped. "Tell me what you want, what you need." Terri backed her against the desk.

"Oh God, Terri. Fuck me."

Terri stroked deep, withdrew her fingers to tease at her opening, before thrusting deep inside again. She continued the rhythm, drawing Sheila higher and higher. Sheila's contractions started squeezing her fingers, gently at first then more tightly. When Sheila started to moan, she quickened her thrusts. Sheila bucked wildly against her hand, nearly screaming as her walls clenched and spasmed, gripping her fingers tightly and flooding her hand. Sheila stopped trembling, and Terri withdrew her hand and licked her fingers. "You taste so good. I can't wait to put my mouth on you. You want that, don't you?"

Terri laughed when Sheila grabbed her by the hand. "Yes. Let's go. Tripod's at my house. You can drive the truck."

Chapter Twelve

SUMMER ARRIVED IN THE mountains, cool mornings, sunny afternoons, and the ever-present mist snaking its way over the mountaintops. Sheila and Terri rode the motorcycle in the evenings or went hiking with Tripod on easier trails. They made little discoveries about each other. Terri rarely watched television, and when she did she preferred mysteries, or if something was bothering her, old kung fu movies. Sheila preferred police dramas. They enjoyed playing cards, gin rummy and poker. Terri took advantage of Sheila's poor poker skills, and frequently had her naked after several losing rounds of strip poker.

They had also discovered that Sheila could not cook on the grill, and that Terri preferred cooking over doing the dishes. They settled into a routine of Terri preparing dinner, and both eating shortly after Sheila got home.

Terri finished washing the pans she had used to prepare dinner and sat down with a glass of wine when Sheila came in. "I'm glad you're still here. I'm sorry I'm so late."

"I'm sure it was important. Are you hungry?"

"Starved."

Terri walked over to the kitchen. "Wine?" She lifted the bottle of white wine she had opened, gesturing with it. "I made some fish, wild rice." She offered a glass of white wine to Sheila, held it an additional moment as their hands touched on the stem. Leaning forward, she kissed her. "Hi there. Welcome home."

"Oh, sorry. Hi." Sheila returned the kiss. "I was afraid you would have left."

"No, I had things underway here, so I stuck around. Do you want to shower while I finish things?"

"Yes, but I'm so hungry."

"Here." Terri moved to the refrigerator and pulled out a shrimp cocktail arranged in a martini glass. "Nibble on this, then shower."

"Oh, Terri, this looks delicious."

"Thanks. What happened that you ran late?"

"A couple brought in their dog. It had eaten something and was bloated. Turned out it was a couple loaves of bread, including the twist ties and wrappers. I had to operate to clear the obstruction." She ate a shrimp, sipped her wine. "Oh, these are tender."

Terri grimaced. "Sounds icky."

Sheila looked over and smiled. "It can be. Did you make this cocktail sauce?" She dipped another shrimp in the thick red sauce. "It's very good."

"Yes. If you sleep with me, I'll give you the recipe."

"I already do. Perhaps we can work out a fair trade for the recipe." Leaning into Terri she nuzzled along her neck. "I'll go clean up. Be back in a few minutes." She ran her hand across Terri's butt before leaving.

By the time Sheila returned the trout almandine and wild rice were ready, along with a salad. Another glass of wine was waiting for her. They ate and chatted about their day. "Business is picking up. It's amazing how many people bring their pets on vacation then let them roam in an unfamiliar place. Bad for them, but good for business."

"Things are getting better then? More clients?"

"Yes, but I'm not out of the woods yet. I'm still afraid I might have to cut one of the ladies' hours. I should have waited on the truck." She sipped her wine. "You don't want to hear this. Let's go outside and watch the sunset."

"Why do you think I'm not interested?"

"It's business. You don't know what it's like to run your own business."

"I don't?"

"No. I'm not only the vet, but I have expenses, property maintenance, utilities, staff salaries, scheduling. If I don't do those too, well, no one gets paid, including me."

"How do you think I get paid?" At Sheila's questioning look, she responded. "You amaze me sometimes. I have to schedule shoots, look at what I can make versus the expenses. If I must travel, I look at the profit potential on that versus if I stayed in the region and worked. I have equipment expenses, taxes. I have a lady who works for me part-time in Charlotte. She helps get me bookings, handles my schedule and checks me on record keeping, taxes. She books my shows. I couldn't do it without her."

Sheila reached out and touched Terri's arm. "I guess I never thought of it that way. I'm sorry."

Terri closed her eyes and took a deep breath. She let it out slowly as she stroked her fingers across her left eyebrow. "Don't apologize. Most people think I jet off to exotic locations and take pictures, but it is a business. I have to keep the clients happy."

"Was your trip to Australia business?"

"It was. I stayed with friends for most of it to help keep costs down. I was able to spend a week up in Queensland in different B&B's."

They walked outside and leaned against the deck railing as the sun slipped lower in the sky. "How did you come to have friends in Australia?"

"I met Alicia and Beth several years ago when they were vacationing in the Keys. I was doing a shoot down there. They watched, asked questions. We got to be friends. They had been working in Georgia for a year. They moved back to Australia about three years ago."

"What were you working on this time?"

"I did photographs for a gay-friendly travel magazine. Alicia works with tourism in Australia. She got me the gig. Beth is a journalist and does a travel blog on the side."

"Do you have a copy?"

"Ah, yes."

"Will you show me sometime?"

"Sure. Have you ever been there?"

"No. Peter would never travel that far. We went to the Caribbean for a few trips. But mostly we went to Aspen, Vale, and Telluride."

"Lots of skiing. I can't picture you as a snow bunny." Terri chuckled.

"I'm a good skier, but they were the only places he would go to for more than three or four days. Turns out his secretary was usually there, too. He could ski better than me, so he would do more difficult trails and I would meet up with him at a certain time and we would ski together the rest of the day. He would go night skiing, too. Encourage me to go for a massage or a spa treatment. He had me fooled. It seems so obvious now."

Terri pulled her close. "They say hindsight is twenty-twenty. Before that, when you were on those trips, did you ever suspect? Even have reason to suspect?"

"No."

"Then don't feel foolish."

"I try not to. I remind myself that he is a very skilled liar, but that doesn't always make me feel better."

Terri took Sheila's hand, and pulled her forward. "Let's go inside, I'll make you feel better."

"Let's. Thank you for dinner."

Chapter Thirteen

SHEILA PACED WHILE TALKING on the phone. "Peter, you're supposed to pay by the tenth of the month. Not the eleventh or the fifteenth. Not half the money, the entire amount. On time."

"If we wouldn't have had a female judge I wouldn't have to pay you anything. You make good money. You can support yourself."

"Unlike you during your residency when I paid for everything!"

"Your parents were helping out. They didn't care how you spent the money."

"The hell they didn't. They expected me to use it for housing and food and education. And yes, they didn't object when you moved in with me. Of course, I paid the bills."

"Oh please, it's not like your parents missed the money."

"Well, you make a whole lot more than my father did in any year so I'm sure you aren't missing the dollars either." She liked being able to throw his own words back at him.

"You're mad because I bought things you didn't get."

"Like the diamond earrings for your secretary? Or maybe the weekends in the hotel with her when you were supposedly on call? You still don't get it, Peter! We were married! The money we made was for us! Not for your mistress. You get to pay because you were stupid enough to cheat and leave a trail of your infidelity using a whole lot of our money. You pay because the judge decided in my favor."

"I still don't think I should have to pay."

"The judge doesn't care what you think, Peter. She was quick to see through your arrogance. You pompous ass."

"I'll send it next month."

"Peter, send the damn check, the entire amount this time, or I'll have the lawyer ask the judge to garnish your wage."

"No, you wouldn't."

"Oh, yes I would." She slammed down the phone. "Dickhead!" Sheila came downstairs from her home office, startled when she saw Terri starting to sit down on the couch. "I didn't know you were here."

"You said six o'clock. I got in a minute ago. I didn't want to interrupt. It's pouring, I didn't want to go back to the car."

"It's okay. Damn, he makes me mad." Sheila walked over and poured a large glass of wine. She started to raise it but was stopped by Terri's hand on her arm.

"Stop. Don't drink when you're mad like this. Tell me what's going on."

"Peter. He's supposed to send me a check every month. It's alimony. He's late again. I have expenses that I need that money for and he has not paid, again." She looked at Terri and saw her furrowed brow, watched her tap her lips. "What are you thinking?"

"I'm wondering, ahh, why he is paying you alimony? You don't have kids. You have your own business, this house."

"He pays because he used our family money to buy gifts for his mistress, take her on trips. I supported us while he finished his training. He repaid me by having affairs. But probably worse than that, he also did everything in his power to keep me from working. To limit my income and control me. He wrote letters to my coworkers and colleagues asking them to decrease my hours supposedly because I wasn't handling the pressure. He was stupid enough to write to my father asking him to persuade me not to work but stay home and be a proper doctor's wife. He sent me multiple e-mails, nagging and cajoling me to only work part-time or not at all. To be a good wife. I had copies of everything. The judge felt that what he had done limited my ability to earn a living, and he must pay. Five years, then he's done paying. That's for the five years he hindered my employment and impacted on my net worth. I need the money to keep the clinic going until business stabilizes."

"That makes sense. I'm glad you got a good lawyer, and a compassionate judge."

"I think I'm going to have to have his wages garnished."

"I understand that happens frequently."

"It will humiliate him."

"He can avoid that by paying on time."

"He could." She poured half of the untouched wine into a second glass and handed it to Terri. "Thanks for listening."

"My pleasure. Can I ask you a question?" Terri held Sheila's hand as they walked to the living room.

"Sure." Sheila sipped her wine and sat on the couch.

"How tight are things at the clinic? I could help."

"Thanks, but no. Absolutely not."

"But—"

"No. I don't want your help. Not financially. Moral support, yes. But that's it." She was frowning, shaking her head.

"Okay. I'm sorry. I wasn't trying to insult you."

"Terri, I need to do this by myself. I appreciate the offer, but no, I can't accept it. I don't want money coming between us. I don't want to worry about paying you back."

Terri crossed to her. "I'm sorry. I didn't mean to upset you."

"It's okay. Let's forget it. How about some dinner? I have some steaks in the fridge, we could grill them if the rain slows down."

"Sounds good. Mind if I cook them though? You can make a salad."

Sheila laughed. "Sure. They won't be tough as shoe leather if you do it."

Roslyn Bane

Chapter Fourteen

WITHOUT EXPLICITLY DISCUSSING IT, their lives started to merge and evolve. They spent the nights together almost always, sometimes at Terri's, others at Sheila's. Terri traveled several times during the month, overnight trips. While away she worked long hours, so she could get back home earlier. Sheila worried as business continued to be erratic. She went out to visit the commercial stables, visited with the few dairy farmers, and traveled to adjacent towns without a veterinarian promoting her clinic.

She spoke with her lawyer about the partial alimony payments and on Peter's efforts to delay the house sale. She called her realtor about the showings on the house, and two offers that they had received. After several calls to her suppliers she was able to negotiate a better price for medications. Perhaps now she wouldn't have to reduce Jamie or Becky's hours. The thought of cutting their hours and affecting their family income was sickening her.

Through it all she tried to stay positive, tried to stay calm, but she felt like she was in the middle of a tornado and her life was spinning out of control. She brought Tripod to her home, not willing to leave the dog alone. The fact was, she cared for the dog and found a strange kind of courage by watching the dog relearn how to do things. She had watched with amused fascination as the dog tried to bury a bone, before finally collapsing onto its belly to dig while lying down.

That's what I need to do. Hunker down, concentrate on the business, and push everything else aside. I have too many distractions, I need to settle into a routine. I am spending too much time with Terri. I'm having fun but I'm not getting my work done. I must get started on the articles on pet care, for the newspaper.

***

Sheila crossed her arms across her chest. "You're going out of town again? Where to this time?"

Terri's mouth fell open and her eyes widened at the anger behind the words. She took a deep breath and answered calmly, "The client didn't like the proofs I sent. I have to meet with them and reshoot if necessary."

"So off you go again." Sheila pushed back from the table, walked over to the kitchen and scraped her barely eaten dinner into the trash. Reaching into a cabinet she grabbed a bottle of bourbon and a glass, poured several fingers worth, and drank most of it immediately. Her hands shook. *Calm down. You're just tired.*

Terri watched, interested and confused by the behavior. "Sheila, my job involves travel. You've known that since before we became involved. It hasn't changed since then. I go where the clients need me. I'm needed in Raleigh."

"Again." Sheila drank, thudding the glass on the counter. "And I'll take care of Tripod again."

"Is that a problem? You don't have to bring her here. Leave her at the kennel if you can't handle her. You're paid for it."

"I can handle her fine. I'm just tired of it."

Terri stood up and crossed her arms. "You're tired of taking care of her specifically, or all animals?" Sheila was silent. "Let your staff do it like they do the other animals. You don't have to get involved with her the way you do. Don't bring her here."

Sheila ran her hands through her hair. "That's not the point."

"Then what is?" Terri took her plate and glass from the table, scraping the rest of her meal into the trash. She rinsed the plates and stacked their dishes in the dishwasher. "Explain it to me, because I don't understand. If you want to break the contract—"

"Damn it, Terri! It's not the dog!" Sheila drained the whiskey glass and shoved it toward the wall and it shattered. "I need something normal, not this traveling all the time, the constantly changing schedule."

Terri jumped, wincing when the glass broke. She pressed a hand against her heart. "It's an overnight. I know it's the third in three weeks, but it happens sometimes."

"Dammit." Sheila placed both hands on the counter and scowled. After several seconds she reached for the broken glass, dropping the larger pieces in the trashcan. "I can't keep it straight. Where are you going to be, when you'll be back? Who are you with? I can't keep up with it." *Stop, you're overreacting. She's not cheating, she's not pressuring you. Calm down. Tell her you're stressed, and that you're worried about the clinic.*

"I'm doing my job. So, I get paid. So, I have the money that I need. Some of which I spend on food, that I cook for you." Terri took the rest of the stir-fry and dumped it in the trash. "And who am I with? What the hell kind of question is that? I'm with a client. And when I'm home I spend as much time as I can manage with you and try to balance that with your need for your own time. I try to support you, my lover, and still give you the space and time to do your work and have some privacy. I try to find ways to make it easier for you to do so. If having someone support you doesn't seem normal, then your marriage was more screwed up than I imagined. I am not your husband. But I'm not your lap-dog either." Terri grabbed her keys and bag. "Sorry if what I do isn't normal enough for you." She walked out, slamming the door behind her.

"Goddamn it!" Sheila pulled at her hair, before slapping both hands on the counter hard enough to make them sting. "Shit! Damn! Fuck!" She went outside and watched the taillights of Terri's jeep disappear around the curve at the bottom of the road. She stormed back inside, slammed the door, locked it, and grabbed the bottle of wine from the table. Swearing as she switched off the lights and stomped upstairs to her room.

***

Terri drove up the long rocky road to her house. Passing her neighbors, she waved to them. There was enough light left that she could get in thirty minutes of cardio to burn off some anger. Parking her jeep, she hurried inside, changing into shorts and T-shirt as Tripod wiggled around her, tail thumping into everything. As she reached for her running shoes, the dog started whining.

"Yes, girl, you're coming, too. Hurry up. Where are your wheels?" She couldn't help but smile as Tripod moved as fast as possible to the closet to paw at the door. "That's right."

Tripod sat, her tail wagging while Terri buckled the harness on and stood waiting while she fitted the harness over her rear quarters. Grabbing the leash, Terri opened the door, stepping out then holding it open for Tripod who scampered down the ramp. She let the dog run free while they headed down the roadway and met her neighbor Jane and her son Tyler coming up.

"Hi, Terri. We were coming up to visit. Tyler wanted to visit Tripod."

"Well, here we are." Inwardly she groaned because she wanted to run, but a little company would be good, too. Besides she knew that Jane's husband Bob traveled frequently. Maybe she could get some pointers on how they made it work. She turned towards Tyler. "How have you been enjoying summer so far?"

"It's okay. Some of it's boring because I don't get to see my friends all the time." Tyler shuffled his feet and looked down at the ground. "My baseball team is good. Maybe you could come watch us sometime."

"I'm sure Miss Terri is busy."

"Oh, I might be able to get to a game. When do you play?"

Tyler smiled broadly. "I play on Wednesday nights and on Saturdays."

"I'll see what I can do, and I'll let your mom know."

Tyler blushed. "Thanks. Can I throw a ball for Tripod?" He pulled a mangled tennis ball from his pocket.

"Tyler, they were going for a walk."

"Please, Miss Terri?"

"Sure, let's go down to your house since we were going that way. It's flatter and your mom and I can talk."

Several minutes later Terri sat on the back porch of a neat ranch house and watched as Tyler threw the ball and Tripod raced after it, wheels bumping along the grass. Jane handed her a glass of sweet tea. "Thanks for stopping. He's been after us for a puppy. A three legged one."

Terri chuckled. "Oh, well that's an interesting twist."

"We're not ready for it. And frankly I couldn't handle a puppy—no matter how many legs—and Tyler, with Bob gone so much."

"I guess it would be tough."

"It wasn't bad when it was only the two of us, or when Tyler was a toddler. But now with Tyler being older it has gotten busier. Speaking of which, it seems you've been busy, traveling a little more lately."

Terri sipped at her tea and wondered if it was on the gossip line that she traveled the last three weeks. "Ah, yeah. It's an occupational hazard, I guess. I have to go back to Raleigh tomorrow for one or two nights."

"Will you be kenneling Tripod again?"

"Yes, I have a contract with Sh-Dr. McDevitt to care for her when I need to travel."

"You know, since it's a quick trip and summertime, we could watch her if you want."

"Oh no, that's sweet but—"

"Tyler would love it. And it will help him see how much responsibility a pet is."

"Are you sure? I would have to show you how to put on the harness and—"

"I'm sure. It will give him something to do besides pester me to take him to the river and ask if his friends can come over."

"Okay, that would be good. I'll give you a key."

"No, just bring her down here."

"Thank you. It's very kind of you."

"Please. It will be fun and very educational for all of us. So, how are you and Dr. McDevitt doing? Sheila, isn't it?"

Terri tried to keep her face neutral, but her heart started to race, sweat breaking out on her brow and back. She sipped at her tea which now tasted sickly sweet. "Ah, um, she's very nice. She's been very kind with Tripod and helping me with her."

"Terri, relax. I was wondering because you seem so happy lately. I was hoping you found someone. I wasn't sure when you first got back if you had met someone locally or when you were visiting your friends in Australia. I was hoping it was here. Australia would be quite a long-distance romance. I've seen you two hanging out together and thought that maybe she was special to you."

"She is." She picked up her tea glass, gestured to it. "Do you have any beer?"

"I think we still have a few of the ones you left here. I'll get you one. Why don't you tell Tyler about tomorrow?"

As Jane went inside, Terri walked over to where Tyler and Tripod now lay in the grass panting. "Tyler, I would like to ask you a very big favor." The boy sat up and looked at her curiously. "I have to go out of town for a few days. Could you take care of Tripod for me, make sure she gets food, and water, and plays catch?"

"Cool. But Mom says that dogs are a lot of work."

"She already said it was okay. But I think you're going to have to help her. Tripod needs someone who can throw the ball far."

"Can I wrestle her?"

"Yes, but you have to take her wheels off first."

He laughed. "That sounds funny. But I will. Mom will help me."

Terri walked back over to the patio. "He's pretty excited. Thanks." She reached for the beer, took a long pull on it. "That tastes good. So how do you do it? The time alone with all of Bob's traveling?"

"Scheduling as much as possible and being flexible when things pop up. I go to bed exhausted sometimes. It helps that it's summer and bedtime can be more flexible. Mornings are too. I don't need to cajole Tyler out of bed for school. It would be hard if I had to work though. We're lucky that Bob makes enough that it's possible for me to stay home." She sipped her beer.

"When Bob comes home, does he help, or does he just want to relax and do nothing?"

"Oh, no! He helps a lot. It gives him time to do things with Tyler, and me some precious alone time—well, not all of it alone." Jane smiled mischievously.

Terri laughed. "I'd hope not."

"Are you tired of traveling?"

"No. It has never bothered me before, and it doesn't now but…"

"But it is hard on a relationship, especially one that's starting out. I don't know Sheila, but she's got to be feeling pressure. The business, a new home, I heard those homes are beautiful inside. She's the new person in town too, with a relationship that some people won't approve of. You both probably feel that needs to be hidden. That's a lot of pressure."

"I know. I try to help but I don't have any idea what I'm doing." At Jane's puzzled look she added, "You know I don't come from a particularly loving or kind family. I'm trying to do things that I think would help but…" She drank from her beer and stared off into the yard.

Jane sipped her beer. "Take your time, ask her how you can help her. You'll figure it out. Can I ask you something? Those women who work down there are sharp. What are you going to do when they realize something is going on between you two?"

"I, ah, hmm. Well, hmm. I hope they leave us alone."

"If you have any trouble with anyone let Bob or me know. I don't know what we could do to protect you other than make sure nobody heads up the hill to hassle you."

"I hope that's not necessary, but it's good to know you have my back."

"You're a friend, Terri, not to mention a damn good neighbor. You're worth looking out for."

They finished their beers, chatting about the upcoming Fourth of July festivities and the annual fireman's carnival. As the last light of the day faded out of the sky, they agreed on a time for her to bring Tripod down in the morning, and she headed up the hill with Tripod leading the way. When she climbed into bed an hour later, she fell immediately asleep.

Roslyn Bane

Chapter Fifteen

SHEILA WOKE AND REACHED for the clock to check the time. "Shit!" Jumping out of bed, she was already in the bathroom before she felt the throbbing in her head. She took two aspirin then showered quickly. She dressed, dashed to the kitchen, toasting a couple slices of bread, and poured a glass of iced tea.

She raced into the office, gave a quick muttered greeting to her staff and went in to see her first patient. Five minutes later, she calmly left the exam room and raced for the restroom to vomit in the commode. The pounding in her head continued, and she splashed cool water on her face.

Using paper towels, she carefully dried off, only then realizing she hadn't put on any makeup. *God! I look a mess.* Pale and clammy with dark circles under bloodshot eyes. *What the hell was I thinking finishing that bottle of wine? And after the double of bourbon.*

Sheila gave herself another moment to make sure her stomach had settled and returned to the exam room. She finished the appointment and got through the next four bookings without being ill again. Glancing at her watch, she went back to her office to enter notes on the visits and listened for Terri's arrival with Tripod. She would have to arrive soon, or she wouldn't be in Raleigh on time. She needed to talk to Terri privately, to apologize and set things straight. She had thought about it last night and decided they needed to slow things down. *I wasn't expecting this. Any of this. This, this thing, relationship with Terri. I'm not ready. Not emotionally. I'm too distracted worrying about the clinic. I need time to get more clients. To get contracts with some of the stables.*

Sheila pulled up a spreadsheet on the computer and grimaced. *Right now, damn it. I'm going to have to pull more money out of my investments.* After a few minutes of online banking were complete, Sheila closed her eyes, leaned back in the chair and let out a long sigh. She almost dozed off when she heard a soft rap on the door.

"Sorry, I didn't mean to startle you. I thought you could use these." Jamie handed her a bottle of water and two pills. "Tylenol, just in case you didn't take anything before." Sheila opened the water and took the pills right away. "Fun night, rough morning?"

Sheila stood looking at her. "I had a bit of a pity party last night and overindulged. I should know better."

"You're human. It's allowed. The Davidsons should be here in about ten minutes. How do you want to handle it? There are eight pups, six weeks old."

"Let's use the large room, and the lift table. We can do each pup on the table or we'll end up wrestling on the floor trying to fend the others off."

"Sounds good. I'll set up the room. This is the first round of vaccines, and worming."

"Thank you. Great Danes, right?" She looked up when the loud commotion of puppies arriving filled the room. "Has Terri brought Tripod in yet for boarding?"

Jamie arched her eyebrows. "No, there was a message on the answering machine this morning when we opened that she would not need boarding this week after all."

"Oh, all right. Let me know when you're ready." Sheila sat back in her chair, closing her eyes and rubbed at her temples. *You were pretty irrational last night. Just tell Terri that you're worried about the business. Tell her that discussing the financial end of the clinic with her makes you feel uncomfortable. She'll understand.* Sheila jumped when the intercom buzzed that Jamie and the puppies were ready.

At lunchtime, Sheila tried to call Terri, but the machine picked up again. She left a quick message. At three she tried again with no luck. After leaving the office, she drove over to Terri's, driving the long narrow drive up the hill. She stopped in surprise when she saw a young boy and his mother playing with Tripod in their yard. She turned off the car and walked over to the fence.

Jane came over and greeted her, "Hi. You must be Dr. McDevitt." At Sheila's look of surprise, she said, "I recognize the car. I'm Jane. Terri's told me about how you saved Tripod." They shook hands.

"Nice to meet you. Tripod is doing well, I see. Does your son play with her often?"

"Tyler. Not as much as he would like. These next few days will be a good experience for him."

"Days?"

"Yes, Terri's letting Tyler get a taste of pet ownership. I am hoping he realizes how much responsibility it is, and he changes his mind about wanting a puppy, at least for a little while." They stopped talking when

Tripod started barking and ran over to them, tail wagging furiously. She tried to nuzzle Sheila through the fence and whined in approval when Sheila reached over the fence and started to scratch behind her ears.

"Hi, Tripod, how are you doing? Where's the ball?" She scampered away and came back with a wet mangled ball. Sheila took it and threw it, sending Tripod racing after it.

"Do you know when she'll be back?"

"I believe Wednesday evening. Is there a problem? Does Tripod need something?"

"No, I wanted to talk to her. I'll guess I'll try later. If you have any trouble with Tripod, you can call me down at the clinic." Sheila took the ball from Tripod. "Sorry, girl, I have to go. Just one more toss." She threw it again and waited for the dog to return. "Bye, Tripod, be good." She patted the dog on the head and turned to Jane. "If you have any problems you know where to find me."

"I do. Terri gave me the clinic number. It was nice meeting you."

"You too. Come see me if you get that puppy." Sheila returned to her car with a smile on her face but inside she was seething. She waited to get down the driveway before letting out a string of obscenities. She dialed Terri's cell phone, cursed when she realized she didn't have a good signal, and finally dropped the phone back in her purse.

She got home and picked up her phone and tried Terri's cell phone once more, which went to voice mail. "Terri, do you think it was necessary or wise to leave Tripod with a young boy? I told you taking care of the dog was not a problem. I'm sorry, I'm tired. And feeling a bit overwhelmed by everything. I should have explained that last night. Please don't ignore my calls. I...I need to talk to you. Please."

***

Terri felt the phone vibrate in her pocket, ignored it, and continued to listen to the client talk about what he didn't like about the photos she had just shot. She listened again to his concerns. Finally, he stopped complaining long enough to take a deep breath and a sip of the now cold coffee, and she spoke. "Mr. Davis, I understand your concerns. I think this will show much better if we use an outdoor location. It's supposed to be sunny tomorrow, so I need to shoot early, between six thirty and eight thirty in the morning, nine o'clock at the latest. That or we wait to the evening, after six when the light starts to soften."

"I can't have the models, makeup, and designers come in that early without warning them. It's too late to call now."

Terri glanced at the clock on the wall. 7:30 p.m. "Okay. Are you in agreement that we'll try this outside?" He nodded. "Good. I would like to start shooting at six in the evening, the weather is supposed to be dry. I'll shoot while I have the light. And then on Thursday morning we'll shoot starting at six-thirty."

"Anything else?" he asked derisively.

"As a matter of fact, yes. I think part of why you're unhappy with the pictures is the makeup."

"The makeup is fine."

"No, it's not. Look at this." She picked up several photos, pointing at different faces. "You want these models, their faces and clothing to stand out from the background models. You have your stars dressed in colors that are clashing with each other and their makeup is being done in such a way that it appears overdone. Let's subdue the background models and tone down your makeup so that they look more natural. They look like they're made up for a stage performance."

He looked at the pictures again and stroked his chin. "Christ, you're right. I guess I am going to have to tell my wife that her niece is overdoing the makeup. This better work, Ms. Greene, because my wife is sure going to make my life a living hell for the next few days because of this."

***

Unable to sleep Sheila looked again at her personal finances and the clinic's finances. Peter sent half the payment, again. Cursing she looked at the clock and realized it was after nine in California. She called and left a message for him to mail the payment and e-mailed her attorney about the latest delay. She then e-mailed the realtor asking if there were any offers on their Virginia home. When she got her share from the house sale, she wouldn't have to worry about cash flow.

While she was at it, she sent e-mails to her siblings and parents. She would rather have talked to them but wouldn't wake them up. Giving up on falling asleep any time soon, she grabbed a magazine. She saw that it was a photography magazine that Terri had left and went into the kitchen to get a glass of wine. Remembering this morning's hangover, she got water instead, and went upstairs to her room.

Climbing into bed she began to read through the magazine. She gave up on trying to understand the technical jargon and looked at the pictures. A feature on what photographers would do to get the perfect shot grabbed her attention. Shaking her head in amazement she looked at photos that someone had taken of other photographers working. Adjacent to the picture was a photograph of what the original photographer was actually trying to capture. Some of the photos showed photographers squeezed into tiny spaces, or atop skyscrapers. Others were crawling through mud, or up in trees. But one photo made her catch her breath. There, in full color was Terri dangling in midair, looking like a spider descending on a string. She was outfitted in climber's gear, eyes bright and focused, a look of concentration on her face. The adjacent photo she had taken was of a raging waterfall, pounding over rocky cliffs.

Several more pages with increasingly stunning photos followed. A second picture of Terri showed her hanging inverted over a crevice, taking pictures of a sandstone formation. Sheila jumped up, dropping the magazine.

"Jesus. Jesus Christ, Terri, what are you doing?" Sheila picked up the magazine again, reading the location. She went back into her home office, fired up the computer, and googled the locations. She became queasy when she read the depth of the crevice and the number of people who had fallen to their deaths there when their lines tangled and broke.

She searched Terri's name on photography sites and read reviews of her work. She found several interviews with her concerning 'Getting the shot.' Sheila found articles from several years earlier listing Terri as one of the up-and-coming photographers to watch. She found awards, honorable mentions, and shows that she was featured in. One article described Terri as being likeable, surprisingly down to earth, and passionate about the Smoky Mountains. It also said that she was elusively silent regarding her past.

"There's a reason for that." Sheila glanced at the clock and groaned. Three in the morning. She shut down the computer and went back to bed. Tossing and turning, she reached over and grabbed another pillow, pulling it in close to her body. She sniffed it deeply, smelling the subtle scent of Terri on it and relaxed. She drifted into sleep, but had vivid, disturbing dreams of Terri hanging over steep cliffs and jagged rocks while inky-black water crashed and roared far below.

Chapter Sixteen

THE NEXT EVENING SHEILA sat in her office finishing the charts for the day. She looked up when she heard someone approach the doorway. She hoped it was Terri. Her heart gave a little dip and she tried to keep the smile on her face when she realized it was Jamie.

"Hi, I didn't know you were here," Sheila said.

"I came back. I was on my way home from the market and saw that you were still here. Is there something wrong?"

"No. I was finishing charts and reviewing the charges. Have to pay the bills."

"Becky does the charges."

"I know but I like to review what's going on. I get a better feel for our expenses that way, too." Sheila was silent for a moment. "Jamie, I hate to say this, but if business doesn't pick up, I'm going to have to cut back hours for both of you. I don't want to lead you on that things are going well. You've both been in this long enough to know when business is bad."

"Have you eaten?"

"What?" She shook her head slightly at the change in topic. "No, not yet."

"I have a couple of frozen dinners in the groceries. I'll bring one in. I have a few ideas I would like to bounce off you. You can eat while I do that. Chicken or fish?"

"Ah, chicken."

"I'll be back."

Sheila pulled up her personal e-mail and saw there wasn't one from Terri. She looked at her phone, fingered the keyboard, and contemplated calling Terri again. She had called several times already but not left messages. She finally admitted to herself that her behavior was getting creepily possessive and she put the phone away. She would have to wait until Terri called.

Several minutes later, Jamie returned. "Here you go." She placed the microwaved entrée in front of Sheila along with a bottle of water.

"This smells pretty good. Thank you. I'll replace it."

"You don't have to. Are you okay?'

"Yes, why?"

"You seemed off today. Tired. Sad."

"I didn't sleep well. I think the stress of moving, getting set up at home and here has finally taken its toll. Not to mention the divorce. It's wearing me down."

"I guess so, it's a lot to handle."

"About yesterday. I want to apologize to you for coming in the way I was. It wasn't very professional. It won't happen again."

"No problem. It's nice to know you're human, too. Hopefully you'll sleep better tonight."

"I hope so, too." Sheila ate some of the chicken. "This is actually quite good."

"They're okay. I have them when my family is out for the day and I don't want to cook."

"That's a good idea. I should get some, too."

"Why? You always have good leftovers."

"That's when Ter...ah, that's because I have a well-stocked freezer." Sheila couldn't help but notice Jamie's raised eyebrows and curious stare. Several seconds of silence passed, "What did you want to discuss?"

"I know you've been worried about the business and income. Becky and I have been too. I think if we update the website it may help. It hasn't been updated in a long time other than putting your name on it. Becky's son is learning website design, he could help refresh it. Terri Greene could probably help."

Sheila stopped eating, her fork in midair. "Terri, how?"

"We should put some new photos up, ones of Tripod, and some of the Dane puppies from yesterday. When folks come, they always ask about Tripod if they don't see her. Even in town Becky and I get questions. The wheelchair gets a lot of comments. Maybe Terri would do the photos."

"Oh. Well I doubt that Ms. Greene would be interested in taking photos of animals, and if she was, I doubt that I could afford her fee."

"But she's your...ah...friend."

"This would be business. She respects us as being a business and pays us for taking care of Tripod. Her business is photography, she should be paid. Besides, from what I've seen, Ms. Greene is a very private person. I doubt that she would want pictures of Tripod all over the web."

"Sheila, can I be frank with you?" Sheila nodded. "You're dating her. I think you should ask her for help. If you want to keep it on a business level, ask to trade a few photos for some free kennel time. Think about it at least."

Sheila was silent for a moment while her heart raced. ""I'll consider it. How do you know that we're dating?"

"At first I didn't. Becky mentioned it. But to those of us who know you, it is obvious you two are. The way you look at each other. Plus, I've seen you in town together."

"It doesn't bother you?"

"No. It doesn't. Becky either. I don't think many people realize it and I don't think you'll have too much trouble. There will be a few, but everyone has skeletons in their closet. If necessary, some of us will rattle those bones until they leave you alone."

"Thank you."

"One other thing. We've gotten calls from people asking about Tripod and the wheelchair. Maybe you should consider taking on more handicapped pets. You know, give people an alternative to putting down the pets. I mean, we're small, we need something different. Something to make us special."

Sheila was quiet for several seconds. "I like it. Let me do some research. I'll need to go through Dr. James' records and see how many dogs were put down for trauma, lost limbs, broken limbs."

"I can do that. I'll see if any of the other clinics around will share their numbers."

"Thank you, this has been really helpful. In fact, I should have talked to both of you about this sooner."

"Probably. But you have your reasons. I hope you trust us."

"I do. This withholding of information is a bad habit I developed. In the past, my ex would use it to try to manipulate me. I promise to work on it. You should get going before your ice cream thaws. Thanks for the dinner."

Jamie smiled. "Good night."

Sheila left fifteen minutes later, her step a little lighter than it had been in several days. After she got home, she started researching for vets specializing in handicapped animals. Several hours later, she took a quick shower before tumbling into bed and was asleep within seconds.

The message light on her phone flashed silently, unnoticed.

***

Terri hung up her phone. Exhausted, annoyed and counting down the hours until she could be back home, she fell onto the bed. She replayed in her mind the messages she had retrieved from her home phone, and the one from her cell phone last night. Sheila was pissed about the dog. Well, Tripod was her dog, not Sheila's. Sheila had seemed upset with the idea of taking care of Tripod again, so she made other arrangements.

She had spoken to Jane last night, letting her know that she was going to be yet another night, and was reassured that they were all doing well, and that the extra night wouldn't be a problem. Terri had already bought a small gift for Tyler, and a bottle of wine for Jane for her trouble.

Sheila's rambling calls on Monday night had become increasingly irate. Obviously, she got quite drunk. One thing came through loud and clear though, Sheila wanted out of the relationship.

Terri punched at the pillow next to her, upset at herself for ignoring her own doubts and pressing forward in a relationship that was doomed to fail. Had failed. She wanted to go home, lick her wounds and let her heart begin to mend. She would have to keep using Sheila's clinic for boarding until she could arrange something else. She would insist that Sheila honor the contract until she could make other arrangements.

With a heavy heart, Terri drifted into a restless sleep. Tossing and turning, she started to whimper in her sleep. Pain seared through her body, it started rapidly and spread through her body in sharp stinging blows. Struggling to breathe as kick after kick landed on her abdomen until she rolled back over to protect herself. She struggled to her hands and knees and crawled across the floor as the blows rained down. The coppery taste of blood filled her mouth, as tears ran down her face. She flinched and cried out as the belt hit her again and again, ripping the flesh on her back, as her parents screamed at her. "You are an abomination, a freak, I hope you burn in hell. There will be no dykes in my house! Get out! Get out! No one will love you ever, you filthy dyke."

She awakened with a shout, drenched in sweat, shaking. She turned on the lights and sat rocking herself on the bed for several minutes as she scanned the room for danger. After several minutes, she started to chill, and changed her shirt before going to the mini fridge to grab a beer. Twisting the cap off, she turned on the television, clicking through the channels until she found an old kung fu movie. She checked the locks on the doors and windows and settled on a chair. There would be no more sleep tonight.

Chapter Seventeen

ON THURSDAY AFTERNOON, SHEILA was surprised when Jane stopped by the clinic asking to speak with her. "Is something wrong with Tripod?"

"Other than she misses Terri, and that she keeps looking up the road toward their house, no. She howled horribly the other day after you left."

"Oh, I'm sorry about that."

"I explained to Tyler that she was missing both of you. I know you're busy, so I'll be quick. Terri called and left a message, there is an accident on the interstate and she is stuck in traffic. I tried to call her back but can't get through. I wanted to let her know we won't be home this evening until late. We'll keep Tripod again if we're not able to make the exchange before it gets too late."

"Okay. I'll see that she gets the message."

"Do you mind if I close the door?"

"Sure."

Jane closed the door while Sheila looked at her curiously. "I've known Terri for five years. She has a good heart. She had a crappy childhood and doesn't trust easily. You must have hurt her the other night. She wouldn't have left Tripod with us otherwise. I don't know what happened, and don't care to, but I'll tell you this—don't think you can use her for a rebound fling to make your ex look bad."

Sheila's mouth dropped open momentarily, and her cheeks grew warm. "I...she...what are you talking about?"

"I know you two are dating, involved. I don't care about your preferences. I care about my friend. I don't like seeing her hurt or used."

Heat raced through Sheila's body and her skin tingled. "I'm not using her. I care for her and I don't see how this is any business of yours. You should leave now." She gestured to the door.

"I'm asking you to be careful with her. She puts on this brave front, but inside she hurts. That comes from her family. Don't let it come from you, too."

"I know about her family and I have no intention of hurting her. As I said, I care for her."

"I hope so because she sure cares for you. I don't mind if I have offended you or pissed you off. She's my friend and she deserves to be loved and treated with respect."

"That's what I'm doing." Sheila deliberately walked to the door and jerked it open, "Leave." She caught the bewildered looks on her employee's faces as Jane left. Saying nothing, she closed the door.

Sheila sat quietly for a few minutes, her breathing gradually slowing as she thought about the conversation. *Wasn't that what Terri had been doing? Taking care of me? What did I do in return? Bitched and complained that I felt crowded and wanted more time to myself. But that's not what I really want. I want things settled, and secure. Good God, have I even thanked Terri for cooking, for buying groceries, and running errands for me? Damn it wasn't shock it was fear when the glass broke. I frightened her. She was afraid of what might happen next. How could I have been so careless? If she'll let me, I'll give her a welcome home she's sure not to forget.*

***

The sun was setting as Terri made the turn onto her road. Yawning, she glanced at Jane's house, and not seeing her car, realized she wasn't home. A few moments later Terri parked her Jeep and grabbed her bags. It felt good as her legs stretched for the first time in several hours. She read the note from Jane on the front door that they would be back later tonight and would bring Tripod up in the morning.

Terri stowed her photography equipment and placed her suitcase on top of the washer. She went into her room, stripping clothes off along the way. She turned on the shower, rummaged through the medicine cabinet and quickly downed two aspirin. As soon as the water was warm, she stepped into the shower.

Terri leaned against the wall, her forehead resting on the tile while the pulsing spray struck her back and neck. She quickly soaped and rinsed but continued to stand and let the water soothe her. She rolled her neck and shoulders, wishing the aspirin would work faster. Minutes passed. Talking out loud, she ran through a list of things she needed to do.

"Download the photos, clean the lenses. Charge batteries. Get Tripod early tomorrow. Get groceries and cut the grass." She thought of

Sheila and shook her head. "That's over. Get it together, Greene."

The water started to chill, she sighed and turned it off. She reached for her towel and frowned when it wasn't there. Stepping out of the shower, she startled when she saw Sheila. "What are you doing here?"

Sheila stepped forward, towel opened, and wrapped it around her and hugged Terri close. "I'm sorry. I've treated you poorly. I've missed you. Let me help you." She pressed her mouth to Terri's, teasing lightly. "You need to relax." Sheila pulled Terri forward. She brought her mouth to Terri's again, the kiss so soft, so delicate, that it drew Terri forward to feel it.

Sheila smiled against Terri's mouth. "Let me do this for you." Terri looked into Sheila's sparkling hazel eyes, saw the determination in them and she tried to relax, tried to enjoy the firm hands as the towel rubbed on her back and arms. Sheila whispered in her ear, nuzzling at her neck. "I love your back, your arms, so strong. I love when they're wrapped around me."

Sheila stepped back, pulling the towel with her. She patted it gently across Terri's breasts, her fingers grazing across the nipples until they peaked. She rubbed the towel across Terri's torso, and slowly moved down to her abdomen, continuing lower, pausing momentarily at her mound to massage the towel softly across it. Terri shivered.

Sheila smiled wickedly before capturing Terri's mouth again. This time the kiss was more seductive. Quick flicks of her tongue teased, enticed, until with a soft moan Terri's mouth opened, yielding, welcoming. After several seconds Sheila broke the kiss and moved down, drying Terri's legs. Kneeling, she lifted each foot, drying it thoroughly. Lowering Terri's foot to the floor, she pushed her back against the counter and nudged Terri's legs apart with her hands.

The counter was cool against Terri's butt and hands as she leaned back. A quick shiver ran through her as warm moist air blew across her sex. Her stomach quivered as a finger traced her outer lips. She watched as Sheila kissed up her inner thighs and groaned when Sheila paused and traced her fingers along the path her lips had taken. She reached out to guide Sheila's head where she wanted it, needed it, but stopped, surprised when Sheila grabbed her hands, placing them back on the counter.

"They stay right there."

Terri whimpered again when warm air blew across her, and gasped when finally—finally—she felt a finger, and then a tongue part her folds, with delicate strokes.

She grew wetter as fingers teased at her opening, drifting upward and skimmed around her clit, not touching it. She shifted her hips, trying to get more contact, and cursed softly in frustration as Sheila passed it by yet again.

A hot moist tongue stroked up the length of her again and again. Terri groaned as a finger probed delicately at her opening before pushing in, slowly penetrating her. She threw her head back with a soft sigh shuddering as lips and tongue stroked and flicked against her clit.

The finger inside her was joined by another. The slow stroking increased and kept pace with the flicking of tongue. Fire burned through her, racing to a flash point, her muscles tense, aching. Sheila pressed her mouth firmly against Terri's sex, gently dragging her lips over her nub and stroked deep.

Terri reached out, grabbed Sheila's head, forcing it against her as she ground against the eager, energetic tongue. She cried out as her body erupted, arching backward and shaking with release.

After a few seconds Terri became aware of fingers continuing to caress her, stroking her sex but bypassing her clit. Teasing bites on each hip, and soft delicate kisses on her abdomen left her wanting more. A trail of liquid kisses led up to her breasts, leaving her helpless. Terri gasped as teeth closed on her nipple, which was immediately soothed with gentle sucking and laving. And still fingers stroked fluidly, languidly into her.

Terri started to rock her hips in time with the probing fingers, tension building in her core. She reached out, pulled Sheila away from her breasts, her hands tight in her sunny-blond hair, and crushed her lips to Sheila's. She could taste herself on her lover's mouth. The kiss was wild, and desperate, and ended with a cry of release.

Propped against the counter, Terri leaned forward, arms draped around Sheila's neck, eyes closed, forehead to forehead, as her breathing calmed, her heart rate slowing. Sheila supported Terri's weight, and kissed her head.

"Feel better?"

Terri laughed softly. "How could I not?" Terri took Sheila's hand, and pulled her toward the bedroom.

Sheila stopped her. "Later, let's get something to eat." Terri smirked at her. "Some food. I made lasagna earlier. It's in the oven staying warm."

Chapter Eighteen

"GO AHEAD I'LL CATCH up with you. You'll be along the river trail?"

"Yes. I already packed Tripod's harness and plenty of water."

"Okay I'll be ten minutes behind you. I'll meet you on the trail near Big Rock Lookout. We can continue from there."

"Sounds great. I'll see you soon." Sheila bent down to kiss Terri, who offered her cheek as she stayed focused on the computer screen.

"Ahem."

Terri looked up. "Oh, sorry."

Sheila lowered her mouth to Terri's and gave her a smoking hot kiss. "Hurry up."

"Oh, I will." Terri set the alarm on her phone for ten minutes. She had just pressed the save icon for her document when her phone alerted. "Okay, I'm going." She hurried to the Jeep and rode off. One mile down the road she noticed the ancient vehicle was handling poorly. She pulled off the road and checked the tires. "Damn! This is not a good time."

It took her ten minutes to change the tire. She texted Sheila to update her. A short while later Terri parked and headed toward the meeting spot. She came to the outcropping of rock and walked out to see if she could spot Sheila and Tripod. After several minutes she spotted them on the bank of the river. She watched as Sheila removed the harness and waded with Tripod into the river. Sheila was keeping Tripod in shallow water as the dog carried a huge stick in its mouth. Terri watched as they played together, and a gentle warmth spread through her body.

She jumped when the sudden blast of sirens filled the valley. She heard Tripod yelp and watched as she pushed by Sheila's arm and moved out to deeper water. Sheila swam after the dog.

"No! No!" Terri screamed. She started running. "Get out! Get out! They're opening the dam." Sweat poured down her back as she ran along the trail screaming. The sirens sounded again. "Sheila, get out of the water." The trail was heading away from the river as it descended toward the valley. Terri fumbled with her phone while she ran. She cursed when Sheila's phone went immediately to voicemail.

***

"Tripod, come on. It was just a siren. Come on. It's okay. Don't be afraid." Sheila reached for Tripod's collar when the sirens sounded again. Tripod yelped and surged away. "Tripod come on." *What's the siren for? Oh shit. They're going to release water.* "Tripod!"

Sheila swam faster and grabbed Tripod by the collar guiding her back to the riverbank. There was two feet of muddy bank before a steep slope of five feet. Sheila looked back at the river and realized she might not have time to find a better place to get to higher ground. A dull roar could be heard drifting through the valley. *Where is Terri?* She tapped her pockets for her phone and remembered placing it in her jacket pocket before setting it on some rocks. *Shit.* A moment later Terri burst through the brush.

Terri dropped to her knees, "They've opened the gates on the dam."

"I just realized that. Here take her."

Sheila lifted Tripod. After several attempts they were able to get Tripod up the embankment.

"Give me your hand." Terri reached down, but their hands were slick with mud and slipped repeatedly. Terri pulled off her shirt to wipe their hands. Sheila grabbed hold of an exposed tree root and started to scramble up the slope. As the root pulled free Terri was able to grab her arm and pull her up. Standing together on the embankment Terri hugged Sheila fiercely.

"Are you okay?"

"Yes. I'm fine. We're okay. I didn't remember at first what the sirens were for. It spooked Tripod. How fast does the water rise?"

"It depends on how far the gates are opened. It will rise faster here because the river is narrow in this section. I tried to call you."

"My phone is in my coat, back up stream. Oh, damn. So is Tripod's harness"

"Let's go see if we can get it. It might be too late."

They moved along the trail, but Tripod could not keep up. Terri asked Sheila to stay with Tripod while she ran ahead to try to retrieve their gear. Five minutes later she reached the rocks that Sheila had left her jacket on and were now surrounded by shallow water. Terri scurried over the rocks and retrieved the jacket and Tripod's harness. A few minutes later Sheila and Tripod arrived. Terri helped Sheila put the jacket over her soaked clothes so she could stay warm. Together they put the harness on Tripod.

Terri took Sheila's hand in hers, "Come on, let's go home."

***

Three weeks later, while enjoying a late dinner outside and watching the sun go down, Terri noticed that Sheila had gotten unusually quiet. Reaching across the table she picked up Sheila's hand. "What's wrong? You haven't said much tonight."

"I need to ask you something. This is very hard for me. It's business, but I am afraid it might interfere with the personal." Sheila got up and started to pace across the deck. Terri sat patiently, watching Sheila move back and forth, trying not to bite at her nails.

After several minutes Terri broke the silence. "Whatever it is, say it. You're making me dizzy moving back and forth like that." She laughed. "You're like a duck moving back and forth in an arcade game."

Sheila braced herself against the railing, her arms crossed loosely in front of her. "I would like you to take some photos around the clinic, of the staff, and some of the animals."

"Okay."

"I need to update the website. Apparently, some of the pets on it have been gone for years. Dr. James never kept up with the website. Wait. What? All right? You'll do it?"

"Of course."

"But I can't pay you. Or at least not your usual fee."

Terri placed her water glass on the table. "My usual fee?"

"I called your assistant and found out your fee. I can't swing that now."

"How long have you been thinking about this?"

"Since you were in Raleigh."

"Three weeks you've been thinking of asking me to take pictures and never asked?"

"It's your business. You get paid to take pictures and I was afraid you would think I was taking advantage of you."

"I think that's a holdover from your time with your ex. I do take pictures. I also do favors for friends when I can." Terri walked over and took Sheila's hands. "Tell me what you need, and I'll decide if it's possible."

"I need a few pictures to put on the website. Current clients. Including Tripod, with her chair." A small crease appeared in Terri's brow. "I know you like your privacy, Terri, but I am going to try to start pulling in more pets that have been injured like Tripod was. Give the animals and their families a second chance. I need a success story or two. People ask about her all the time."

"They do?"

"Yes. She's been there enough that people look for her. Surely people have asked you about her when you walk her in town or on the trails?"

"Yes, they do. I never paid much attention to how often. I thought they were being polite."

"We've tried taking pictures in the office but they're, well, snapshots." Sheila shrugged. "I understand if you don't want to. It is your business. I won't be upset if you don't want to do it."

"I'll do it. On one condition."

"Which is?"

"We go kayaking over the Fourth of July weekend. We'll stay local. I would like to camp but it's not possible to kayak and camp with Tripod too. If it was only camping, I would take her."

Sheila bit lightly on the inside of her cheek and tilted her head "Kayaking? You're serious?"

"I am. The area is famous for it. Or haven't you noticed all the colorful boats on top of the cars and in the rivers?" Terri smirked.

"I've never done it. I don't think I can."

"I'll teach you. Besides, the locals need to see you do something they do."

"Can't I go to the fireman's carnival?"

"You're going to do that, too."

"Geez, Terri, I don't know."

Terri cupped Sheila's cheek, and gave her a feather light kiss. "If you're afraid, you don't have to. I'll do the photos no matter what."

"I am. What if I turn over? How do you get out?"

"I'll show you. Let's go to one of the lakes on Saturday. We'll go where it's shallow and flat water, I'll teach you some of the basics." Sheila looked doubtful. "Trust me, sweetheart."

"Okay."

"I'll make arrangements for Saturday around ten o'clock. Now, let's go inside, I'll give you your first lesson, it's called a wet entrance."

***

Saturday was sunny, warm on the verge of being hot. Sheila stood on the bank and focused on the calm water, which was in direct opposition to the butterflies that fluttered in her stomach. Pressing her hand to her abdomen, she tried to find something positive to say. "I can see the bottom."

"Yes. It's only about three feet deep in this cove. Out there it gets much deeper. Here, put on your life vest and helmet then get in. I'll check the position of the foot rests after you get situated."

Sheila donned her equipment while Terri leaned into the kayak and looked down the long length of those luscious legs. She stroked them and smiled when Sheila gasped. "Sorry, I couldn't resist." She withdrew her hands and looked back in to ensure that the foot brackets looked correct. "Is that comfortable for your feet and knees?"

"I think so."

"Take your paddle, the way I showed you. Good. Now I am going to push you into the water. This part will be like the canoeing you've done before. I'll make sure you're steady then I'll come out and we'll practice what's called a wet exit."

Sheila laughed. "If it's anything like the other night, I am going to enjoy this. But we'll need a little more space than a kayak."

Terri leaned over, nipped at Sheila's ear, and whispered, "I loved hearing you beg." She straightened. "Ready? Here we go." She pushed Sheila smoothly into the water. "Find your balance point. Steady," she said when Sheila wobbled, then settled. Terri walked into the waist-high water.

"I'm going to show you how to get out if you tip. This is not an Eskimo roll, that's an advanced move. This is how you get out after you have flipped over and are upside down. First thing we're going to do is I am going to flip you over. I want you to count to five, tap the side, and I'll roll you back up. Breathe out through your nose so water doesn't go up there. Ready?"

"Um, I guess."

"Stay there for five seconds. Tap. And I'll lift. Soon as you tap, I'll bring you over. Ready? One, two, three." Terri flipped the kayak, counted herself. At five seconds there was a tap and she righted the boat. "How was it?"

"Dark. I think I had my eyes closed."

"That's okay. You feel all right?"

"I'm good."

"This time, once you're under I want you to lean forward as far as you can and put your hands on the front here. Stay under as long as you feel comfortable. Slide one hand to the side and tap. I'll bring you up."

"Why?"

"You'll see in the next step. Ready?" Sheila nodded. "One, two, three." Terri waited, counted to herself. At twenty there was a tap and she flipped the boat upright. Sheila came up coughing.

"Are you okay?"

"Yeah, I got some water up my nose. I hate that. And the water is getting gritty." The silt bottom was getting stirred up with their movement.

"Oh, there's a nose clip on your vest. I forgot to tell you. Sorry."

"Do you use one?"

"I did when I was learning to roll. Not now though. After all, you don't know when you're going to flip and won't have time to put it on. I know some paddlers who wear it the entire time they're on the water. Use it if you want to."

"I'll try without it."

"Your choice. Time to try again. This time, lean forward again, run your hands up along the side of the boat to the front, grab this loop and pull it hard toward you. Slide your hands back to near your hips and push up. You will pop out. If you get stuck, tap. I'll bring you up."

"Can we go through it again?"

"Let's do it without the flip. Close your eyes, lean forward, run your hands forward. Good. Find the loop. Now pull toward you." Sheila pulled the loop and the rubber skirt popped off. "Now run your hands back to near your hips. And you push up. Good. Now put the skirt back on. Make sure the loop is out." She watched carefully as Sheila repositioned the neoprene rubber covering the kayak opening. "Good. Ready?"

"Give me a second."

Terri waited patiently. "You're doing fine. Thank you for trying." She placed her hand on Sheila's chin and drew her in for a quick kiss.

"Mmm. Can I have another kiss for luck before I do this?"

Terri steadied the boat, leaned in and gave her a feathery light but lingering kiss. She pulled away. "That's all until later. Ready?" Sheila nodded and after a count of three she flipped her. Five seconds later, Sheila popped up outside the boat.

"It worked!"

"Of course, it worked. That was fast. Get in and do it again but stay under a little longer before you pull the skirt off. Get used to being under. Don't panic. Work through the steps. Tap if you need help."

Sheila walked the boat over to more shallow water, got back in, and paddled back to Terri. "Let's do it. Flip me when you're ready. Surprise m—"

Terri flipped her over. Twenty seconds later Sheila emerged a huge smile playing across her face. "That was fun. One more time, please?"

Sheila set up again. Terri flipped. Silt rose in the water. At thirty seconds, Sheila hadn't popped up. With her heart in her throat, Terri righted the boat and had a split second to realize Sheila wasn't in it. Panic and confusion rose as Sheila's life vest and helmet floated to the top. In the split second it took to react—before she could dive under to look for her—she realized Sheila had popped up behind her. She turned, and it took her another full second to realize Sheila was topless. Sheila grabbed Terri and pulled her over and under.

They wrestled in the shallow water, laughing, hands pushing, pulling, before settling into gentle strokes, quick tugs on nipple and possessive kisses. Terri lowered her mouth to capture a nipple, but jumped, catching movement out of the corner of her eye.

"Oh, shit!" Sheila sank back down in the water, turning away. She scrambled to find her bathing suit top.

Terri stood blocking Sheila from view. The kayaker—a woman, her eyes wide, and mouth open—sat almost motionless, her kayak barely drifting. After a moment she broke into a huge grin. "Sorry to interrupt. I wasn't expecting that last wet exit."

Terri, relieved, smiled back, the woman wasn't angry. "Me either. I can't take her anywhere."

Sheila, blushing furiously, bathing suit top back in place, playfully slapped at Terri's arm. "I'm sorry. I thought we were alone, it seems so isolated here."

"It is. Right here. Right now. But around that corner," she pointed with her paddle, "are about twenty other kayakers. A bus just unloaded on the far side for lessons." Terri and Sheila looked at each other. It was better to be interrupted by one than twenty. "Are you from around here?" the woman asked.

"Not too far away," Terri answered vaguely. "Are you visiting?"

"No. I got stationed here about a month ago. It's my first chance to get out on the water."

"Stationed here? What do you do?"

"I'm with the state highway patrol." Terri flinched at the comment and heard Sheila's muttered curse. "Don't worry. I'm off duty. It's not like I am going to arrest you." She smiled when Sheila sighed and looked at both women. "How long have you been together?"

Sheila was silent, but Terri was intrigued by the woman's questions. "A couple of months. Why?"

"I haven't met anyone with my preferences. I was beginning to think no one gay lives out here in the sticks. Is there a club, or bar where people can meet?"

"There are a couple local bars that are friendly enough. The bars at the paddling resorts are your best bet though. People come in from all over."

"Good to know. Hopefully we will run into each other again. Have a good day."

Sheila and Terri watched as she started to paddle away. With an aching feeling in her gut, Terri called, "Wait! We were getting ready to have some lunch. Why don't you join us? We have plenty."

"Are you sure?"

"Yes." Terri turned to Sheila, whispering as they pulled Sheila's kayak on shore. "We both know how it feels to be the new person in town."

Sheila nodded. "Okay." She reached up and stroked Terri's cheek with the back of her hand. "You have a good heart." She went into the water, swimming over to where her helmet and life jacket bobbed and brought them back to the shore.

The woman pulled her kayak up on the bank and took off her protective gear. She pulled a gear bag out from the cargo hold. Setting her belongings on the picnic table near them, she introduced herself. "I'm Abby Brown."

They shook hands. "Terri Greene." She gestured to Sheila as she walked up to them. "The topless mermaid here is Sheila." Sheila blushed, and they shook hands.

"Nice to meet you. Are you really with the Highway Patrol?" Sheila asked.

"I am. Four years now. This is the first time I've been stationed in this part of the state. It's pretty and not nearly as hot as the coastal areas. It seems a bit more relaxed."

"Traffic doesn't suck either." Terri started to pull food out of the cooler she had set near the table earlier.

"So true."

Terri handed a bottle of wine and a corkscrew to Sheila. "Will you pour?" She placed several cups on the table then brought out plates and cutlery. She pulled out a huge container of salad, grilled, sliced chicken breasts, and a small container of fruit and cheese with crackers.

Sheila chuckled, "My God, Terri. Did you think we were going to starve?"

"Hey, I didn't want us to be hungry. Kayaking can work up quite an appetite."

Abby pulled from her gear bag several peaches, plums, and a huge brownie. She noticed the two women looking at her and raised her eyebrows, "I like chocolate."

They sat down to eat, and talked about the local area, and watched as a steady caravan of kayakers entered the cove. An hour later, after exchanging e-mail addresses, Abby left.

Terri reached out and took Sheila's hand. "I hope you don't mind that I asked her to join us."

"No, I don't. She seems very nice. You were right. It is lonely to be the new person, not knowing anyone around."

"I knew you would understand. Let me go put this cooler back in the Jeep, and we can go out and do some exploring. You can get used to maneuvering a kayak. These are whitewater kayaks, they are very quick to turn, which you need on the river. Then next week we'll hit the river."

They spent the next few hours paddling on the lake, exploring the inlets, and practicing moving between downed trees. After loading the kayaks into the Jeep, they started for home.

"Did you like it?"

"I did. It's easier to maneuver than a canoe." Sheila hesitated. "Abby seems nice."

"Yes, she does. You did great getting out of the kayak when it was inverted." She laughed. "You sure did surprise me the last time you came up." She reached over and stroked Sheila's leg. "You made me forget where we were."

Sheila flashed a quick smile. "I didn't see Abby come into the lagoon. How long do you think she was there?" Terri shrugged. "I wonder what brought her out here? She said job transfer, but it seemed like something else. There was a touch of sadness in her eyes."

"I didn't notice. I thought she seemed friendly. Happy. How did you feel when you were upside down? After you did it a few times, did you feel better or just on the edge of panic?"

"The first few times I was nervous. But it went well. You're a good teacher. Thank you." Sheila leaned over and pecked Terri on the cheek. "It didn't sound like Abby had a girlfriend."

"Huh? I don't know. It sounded like she just moved to the area. She might have someone back on the coast." She noticed the puzzled look on Sheila's face. "She said she was from the coast."

"Oh, that's right. But she did ask where she could meet people."

Terri slowed as she approached town. "Did you have fun today? Do you want to do it again?"

"I did have fun. Thank you." Terri pulled into a parking lot and Sheila looked up surprised. "We're stopping?"

"I have to return your kayak. Are you okay?"

"Yes. My arms are a little sore. It took me a little while to remember to use my torso not my arms."

"We'll be back home soon. Take a long shower or a bath. I'll give you a massage."

"That'll be nice."

After they got back, Terri unloaded her kayak, cleaned it, and put it away while Sheila let out Tripod, played with her and fed her before being joined by Terri. "Why don't you go in and get cleaned up? There's aspirin in the medicine chest. I'm going to take Tripod for a walk. I'll be back and get some dinner started. While it cooks, I'll give you a massage."

"Okay." Sheila turned and hesitated. "Terri? Did you like her?"

"Who? Abby? Yes, she's nice. It was interesting hearing about some of her adventures so far."

"That's not what I meant."

Terri looked at her, saw the unexpected insecurity, the vulnerability so clearly set on her face. "Oh my God! No!" She took Sheila by the shoulders. "Absolutely not. I wasn't trying to get anything started. I won't cheat on you, sweetheart. I hope I never give you reason to doubt that."

Chapter Nineteen

SHEILA GROANED AS SHE rolled over in bed, plumped the pillow and pushed the sheets down. A few minutes later she rolled back over and pulled the sheets back up. Finally, she climbed out of bed.

A light switched on and Terri got up. "Sweetheart, what is it?" Terri handed Sheila her robe and pulled a T-shirt on.

"I can't relax. I'll be okay." She sat on the loveseat and ran her fingers through her hair. "Go back to sleep. I'll be fine."

"Did Peter miss a payment again?"

"No. He was actually on time." She looked up at Terri and took a deep breath. "I'm worried about this trip. You probably think I'm silly. What if I flip and can't get out?"

"You're not silly. First off, the river this time of year only has stage one and two rapids. Stage one can take inner tubes fine. Stage two is still tame. It's not that you can't flip, but the water isn't raging. You know how to wet exit. I'll be there if you get into trouble. If you panic and don't tap, I'll still be there. Is that what this is about? Do you think this is because of what happened with Tripod in the river?"

"No. It was about you."

"Me?"

"Yes." Sheila got up, picked up a magazine, flipped through the pages and handed it to Terri. She looked down and saw the photo of herself hanging inverted over the crevice between sandstone formations. "I keep thinking about you falling down into that, or you end up crashing into dark, black, inky water, full of rocks and boulders. Why would you do that? Just for a picture?"

Terri closed the magazine and placed her hands on Sheila's shoulders. "It is my job. If I thought it was unsafe, that my gear wasn't right, I would not have done it. The team that was with me wouldn't have let me do it."

"I know you take risks—"

"Educated risks."

"They're still risks. And I can't help but ask myself, if you would do that," she pointed to the magazine, "have that kind of courage, what, if anything, would scare you on the river? Maybe your idea of reasonable risks doesn't match mine."

"Oh, baby, I would not expose you to that type of risk. This is a gentle river to paddle on. It's popular with families, I promise. I would not do anything to hurt you or intentionally put you in a situation that is dangerous. Let's drive by a section tomorrow so you can see it. If it's too much we can go elsewhere or cancel it. Whatever you want."

"You would do that?"

"I would."

Sheila took several deep breaths. "Thanks. I think I can sleep now." As they got back into bed she asked, "Terri, you don't do stuff like that very often, do you? Dangling, upside down, or off the edge of cliffs?"

"Not too often. Shh, now. We both have to get up early."

Terri lay quietly listening to Sheila's breathing slow and thought about the fact that someone was worried about her. It was comforting and foreign at the same time. She drifted to sleep with a smile on her face.

***

July Fourth was a beautiful day. Eighty degrees and sunny with humidity low enough that it didn't make one feel like they were suffocating with each breath. The river was crowded with a rainbow flotilla of kayaks, canoes, and occasional inner tubes. As they put on their gear, Terri watched Sheila and saw a little muscle tremor.

"Are you nervous?"

"A little. But it's not like it was the other day when we were here to check it out. Having all these people around is reassuring."

"Good. It's supposed to be fun." Terri looked around cautiously and snuck a quick kiss. "If you get tired, want to stop, or aren't having fun, let me know."

"I will. Let's do this"

"I'll check your gear." Terri ensured that Sheila's life vest was fastened correctly, and that her helmet was snug. She checked the foot rests, made sure her water bottle was strapped down, and watched as Sheila fastened the skirt over the cockpit. "Do you remember how to read the river for submerged obstacles?"

"Yes. I want to look for ripples or the water lifting."

"That's right. First thing we need to practice is how to cross the river. It's called ferrying. This allows you to move from bank to bank, slow things down and make turns. It also allows you to get into an eddy and take a rest while still in the boat." Terri checked her own gear, climbed in, and secured the spray skirt. "Let's paddle out, but I want you to paddle upstream. Like you're trying to move upriver. See that rock over there? There's a shallow area right in front of it. It's out of the current. That's where we want to get. Once you're stable, I want you to angle about forty-five degrees toward it. Look at that rock but keep paddling upstream. It will help if you lean a little to the downstream side. Just a little though. Remember, torso, not arms to stroke."

She watched as Sheila took a deep breath. "Okay. Here I go."

Terri stayed with her, encouraging her, offering several suggestions while she crossed the river. Several minutes later they were across the river.

"That was harder than I thought it would be."

"You did fine. Just watch your angle. If it's too much, you'll turn downstream. That's not a big deal now because the water isn't rough or fast. But if there is an obstacle you can't handle, and you miss your goal...I'll just say your day will get a lot more interesting."

"I bet. Um, we won't have that problem, will we?"

"Not here, not today. Are you ready to try some more?"

"Yes."

"Okay. This time you're going to enter the current. So, start like you're ferrying back across, but as you enter the main current, let the water push the bow around, pull the paddle in close to pivot around it and lean downstream. That will turn you around and you'll be heading in that direction. See that next rock? Once you get past it you should notice the water slowing some. I want you to angle in about thirty degrees, stroke hard once or twice. As you enter the eddy, the river will force the back of the boat around. You'll be facing upriver but in the shelter behind the rock."

She looked at the confused look on Sheila's face. "Watch me. I'll explain what I'm doing. Then I'll come back."

Sheila watched as Terri performed the maneuvers, and then paddled back up to her. "You made it look easy."

"I've done it before. Lots of times. Be patient, take your time and feel what is happening. I'll be right beside you."

"I won't tip?"

"Well, don't lean too far. If you do, remember to pull the loop on the skirt like you practiced. I'm right here. I'll flip you back up if I need to."

"That's reassuring." Sheila rolled her neck.

Terri smiled. "You're doing fine. You did great last week. Relax, feel the water as it moves by the boat."

After several attempts, Sheila was able to do the technique with minimal effort. Terri noticed a smile start to return to Sheila's face as she gained confidence and relaxed. "See, that wasn't so bad. Do you want to rest or head down river?"

"Let's head down."

"Okay. Don't forget you have a water bottle in there with you, remember to drink. A little further down river there will be a big bend in the river, with a beach area on the left. People might be swimming so be alert. While we head down, practice what you just did."

"Okay."

Terri stayed close by, as Sheila practiced, and offered advice if asked. Unnoticed, she took a small waterproof camera out of her vest pocket and took a few photos. An hour later they beached the kayaks and waded in the water for a few minutes before having a snack and drinking water.

"Are you enjoying this?" Terri asked as they sat down on the hull of the kayaks.

"I am. I was worried, but now I'm feeling better about it."

Terri smiled. "Good. When we go back out, I want to show you how to get off a rock if you get pinned against one. We'll practice it until you can get free." Sheila's brow furrowed. "Let's start up here where the water is slower and there's lots of room. If you're going to tip today, now's a good time to do it."

Sheila dragged her teeth across her bottom lip. "I'll keep that in mind."

Terri moved over to sit next to Sheila. She massaged her neck and shoulders. "Relax. See that rock there?" She pointed to the middle of the river where a large rock protruded about a foot above the water. "You're going to hit that rock broadside on purpose."

"Why would I want to do that?"

"So you can practice getting off. Later today we are going to have a few little rapids. You might end up pinned to a rock. If you do the wrong thing, then you will go under."

"Terri, I don't know. If…"

"I'll do it first. You'll see. Are you ready?"

"I guess."

Terri reached over and took Sheila's hand. "Do you trust me?"

"Yes. My own skills...not so much."

"You'll do fine. That's why we're practicing here."

"Okay."

They climbed back into the kayaks, and after double-checking their gear, ferried across the river. Sheila moved into the shelter behind the rock and waited for Terri.

"Watch, and I'll walk you through what I'm doing." Terri came downstream then turned the boat to hit the rock sideways. "If you realize that you're going to come up against a rock sideways, lean into the rock, not away from it. When you come to a stop, pinned against it, use your arms to walk yourself down the rock. Don't lose your paddle. You might have to jump a little with your hips." She demonstrated pulling herself down the rock until she was free. "See? Not too hard. If the water is faster, you have to work harder."

"It seems like you should lean away from the rock, so you don't hit it as hard."

"Nope. No matter what, you're going to hit it. Think hug the rock."

"Can you show me again?"

"Absolutely."

Terri demonstrated the maneuver a couple more times. Finally, Sheila was ready to try. She intentionally steered the kayak onto the rock and leaned into the impact. The water held her pinned and she used her hands to try to push herself off but got nowhere.

"Don't push back, the water has too much force, pull yourself along the rock forward or backward."

Sheila pulled herself along until she was free. "That was harder than it looked."

"It can be, that's why we practice where the water is slower."

"I think I better try it again."

This time, as Sheila approached the rock, she came in faster than before and a split second before impact she shied away, leaning the boat upriver, and was instantly underwater.

"Shit!" Terri shouted. She stretched out across the rock, grabbing the far side of Sheila's kayak and heaved just as Sheila popped up outside the kayak. "Are you okay?" Terri found the guide rope at the end and pulled the kayak close.

Sheila coughed twice. "Yes." She swam around the side of the rock and grabbed her kayak. "How do I get back in?

"Lucky for you there's a little gravel bar right over there, go on over and get back in. It's shallow there." Terri watched as Sheila got positioned in the kayak and saw her hands tremble as she attached the skirt. "Sheila, are you okay?"

"Yeah, I just need a minute." Sheila rubbed her hand through her hair to hide the muscle tremble.

"We can stay here until you're ready. Do you know what you did wrong?"

"I leaned away."

"You did."

"I turned over before I knew it was happening."

"Did you hit your head?"

"No."

"When you're ready we'll head down river. It's only about fifteen minutes if we head straight through. There's a nice area there to have lunch and rest."

"That sounds good."

***

They beached their kayaks on a large cleared bank that had dozens of people enjoying a break. Sheila took off her gear while Terri pulled their lunch out of the hatches. As Sheila stretched, she realized someone was staring at them. "Hey, Terri? Do you recognize that woman near the red kayak? She's looking at us."

"Huh? Where?"

"By the big tree."

"I don't see...hey, wait, it's Abby." Terri waved, and they walked over to her. A man who was next to Abby stood up also.

"Hey, Terri. I wasn't sure if that was you and Sheila. This is my cousin Rob from Roanoke. He's visiting for a few days." They shook hands with him. "Great day, isn't it?"

"It is fantastic. We were going to have some lunch, then relax for a little while."

"We're doing the same." Abby looked Sheila up and down. "Sheila, did you flip? You look soaked."

"I did. Terri was showing me how to get free from rocks and I didn't do it right."

Terri interrupted, "You did the first time."

Sheila smiled. "I did. The second time I was under before I knew it. It startled me, but I did the wet exit and cooled off." Sheila felt a blush

122

rising when she saw Terri try to hide a laugh as she recalled the first night Terri introduced her to the kayaking term with a very different outcome. "Ah, um, so do you want to join us?"

"Sure."

As they ate lunch together, they found out that Rob was a Virginia State Trooper. "Is being in law enforcement a family thing?" Sheila asked.

Rob laughed. "The blue line runs deep in our families. Abby and I broke it a little by joining at the state level instead of an urban department."

"It was such a disappointment to our families. But they've come around. Rob's even allowed to visit his family again," Abby said.

Rob smiled. "Yeah, Dad was pretty upset but he knows I like the rural areas better."

Sheila noticed that Terri was quiet during the exchange, perhaps the talk of family had her feeling vulnerable? Either way, she redirected the conversation. "So how far are you going today?"

"We're camping out tonight and going to continue further down tomorrow."

"We've got about two more miles to go. But there's no rush. We can take it as slow as we want," Terri said.

They finished eating lunch, cleaned up, and then put on their protective gear. Terri stowed the leftovers and trash in the hatches and checked to see if Sheila had her spray skirt on correctly.

The foursome headed downriver together, practicing their skills and enjoying each other's company. Pictures were taken, water battles were fought, and lost. Sheila watched awed as the other three practiced their Eskimo rolls. An hour later Rob and Abby headed downstream to be sure they would get to their campsite before it got too late.

***

Seven hours after they started, they loaded the kayaks onto the jeep and drove back upriver to where Sheila's truck was parked. They caravaned back to Terri's, unloaded and cleaned the gear while squirting Tripod with the hose.

"Hey, why don't you go clean up while I put dinner together? It won't take long, I have meat marinating for kabobs and need to load the skewers. Are you tired?"

"I am. That took a little more out of me than I expected."

"Let's stay here tonight. Forget about going into town for the evening festivities."

"That sounds good. I didn't want to be a party pooper."

"Not at all. A little rest sounds good. I'll finish up here. Go on in. I'll give you first crack at the hot water."

"Thanks. I won't be long."

Terri stowed the kayaks and hung the life vests up to dry. After a few minutes of playing with Tripod, she went inside. She smelled the subtle scent of soap in the air as she entered. Surprised that Sheila was done showering, she walked in the bedroom and found her asleep on the bed. Smiling, she went into the bathroom, showered quickly, and then lay on the bed next to her. In moments, she was asleep too.

***

Terri awakened to Tripod's barking. A boom sounded, and Tripod's barking became more frantic. Terri pulled on some clothes and went outside to calm the dog. "You don't like that noise, do you? Let's go inside." As she opened the door to let Tripod in, Sheila joined them.

"Dogs usually don't like loud noises like that." Sheila knelt and ruffled Tripod's fur. "You'll be okay, Tripod."

"Yeah. I think she'll be inside the rest of the evening. You look more rested."

"I am. Sorry I fell asleep on you."

"I slept too. I only got up a minute before you. Hungry?"

"Starved."

"I never got the kabobs put together."

"I'll do it if you want to start the grill."

"There's a pasta salad in the fridge."

"I'll find it. Do you want wine or beer?"

"There's a chardonnay cooling, I'll go with that."

Terri went out to light the grill. As the coals burned down, she set the table outside and pulled the chaise lounges down into the shade. Going back inside, she opened the wine, pouring them each a glass.

"Coals will be ready in about twenty minutes. Come outside and relax. I put some lawn chairs out." Tripod followed them to the door, but when another boom sounded, she stopped and went over to her bed. "She doesn't like that. Why do people have to start setting off fireworks so early? It's not like you can see them yet."

"Lots of dogs run off when they hear that. She'll do better in here."

They settled into the chairs and Terri sipped her wine. "Did you like the trip?"

"I did. Flipping wasn't much fun, it scared me. It seemed like I was under for a long time, but I know I wasn't."

"Maybe ten seconds."

"And you were right there. Thank you." Sheila leaned over and kissed Terri. "I would like to do it again, it's a nice way to spend the day. I used to spend a lot of time outdoors, but Peter didn't like to. It was easier to do something more sedate than deal with the arguments. Skiing was always fine. But water skiing became just boating. Riding around showing off to his colleagues. It got to the point that I didn't even bother to go out on the boat. I was a waitress to his pals."

Terri sipped her wine and listened quietly as Sheila spoke, letting her tell her story. She said nothing but thought plenty about Sheila's ex, and not much of it was good. She looked up when Sheila quieted. "What's wrong?"

"I was rambling. I didn't mean to vent everything to you."

"It's okay. It's nice to know you do like doing more active things. You've fallen out of practice. If you want to try something, let me know. I'll help if I can."

"Do you think I could learn the Eskimo roll?"

Terri smiled. "Yes. It's best to learn on the lake, though." At Sheila's little frown she asked, "What's wrong?"

"Oh, I was hoping you could show me parts of it today. You know, like when you showed me that wet entrance."

Terri laughed. "Maybe later. After we eat. I think the coals are ready." She stood up and stretched. "How about if we stay up here tonight? We should be able to see the fireworks from town fine."

"We can make our own."

Terri leaned down over Sheila, captured her mouth in a hot greedy kiss and broke it when they were both breathless. "I'm sure we will."

Chapter Twenty

SHEILA LEANED IN, KISSING Terri lightly. "That smells great. What is it?"

"Chicken pot pie. Homemade." She saw Sheila's grimace. "You don't like chicken pot pie?"

"It's not a favorite. It just always tastes like box."

Terri laughed. "Well, this is homemade. There is no box. I think you'll like it, and if you don't, I'll whip up something else for you. How was your day?"

"Good. We're starting to get a few more visits. We're receiving more calls. Several are about Tripod. She's been good for business. Can I charge my phone?" Terri nodded and poured wine for them. Sheila pulled her charger from her purse. "Oh, here, I found this outside. You must have dropped it."

Terri took the envelope from her, read the return address. Her heart stuttered. She quickly put the envelope upside down on the counter. She took a sip of wine and busied herself in the kitchen.

"Terri? That's from New York. Don't you want to open it? It looks like a personal letter."

"Well then, it's personal."

Sheila frowned at the rebuke. "Yes, it is. And you were fine until I gave it to you, now you're closing up. I'll take this nice glass of wine outside and when you decide what you're going to do with that letter, come get me. Come on, Tripod. Let's go outside." She held the door while the dog hobbled over.

Damn. Terri stood looking at the envelope. *It's not a big deal. Just open it.* She finished her wine, filled her glass again, sat, and after taking a deep breath, opened the letter. A photo fell out. She looked at it for a moment, searching for recognition, and then gasped.

While reading the letter, she finished her wine. She put the letter aside and ran her hands over her suddenly chilled arms. She sat for several minutes, her foot bouncing on the floor as she rubbed at her neck. She filled her wine glass again and went out on the porch. Sitting next to Sheila, she took her hand, squeezing it gently. "I'm sorry I was short with you."

"Is it from your family?"

"No, actually. It's from Laurie, we've kept in touch. She moved, and I didn't recognize the street address, just the town. Everything is okay. Come back inside. Dinner is ready." They ate dinner reviewing their day and making plans for the weekend. Terri tried to pay attention, but her thoughts kept drifting back to the letter.

Clearing the table after the meal, Sheila saw the photo on the counter. "Who is this?" She studied the photo. "This man looks like you, it's the eyes. Looks like a nice family."

Terri took the picture, placed it back in the envelope. Pouring more wine, she said, "Looks like it. Do you want to watch a movie or—"

"Terri, come on. I thought we were past this. If there is something in that letter that has upset you, why won't you share it? Let me help you, or at least give me a chance to listen."

"I don't want—"

"I know that. You have no problem getting me to talk about my past, my family, my life, but whenever I try to do the same, you put up this wall. Why don't you trust me? I know you said you're not close to your family, and baby, I've seen the scars, and understand that, but you have scars on the inside, and you never talk about them. Telling someone will help you heal. Let me help you."

"So, you're a psychologist now, too?" Terry pushed back.

Sheila sighed in disappointment and walked away. She hesitated only a moment to pick up her bag. "All right, Terri, you win. Watch your movie, drink a few more glasses of wine. Keep everything bottled up inside you. I've got things to do at home which will be less frustrating than trying to get you to open up about what's hurting you. Thank you for dinner. It was lovely."

Breathing hard, Terri stood in the empty kitchen and listened to Sheila say goodbye to Tripod and start her truck. She cursed out loud, slammed her hands on the counter, grabbed the letter, ran out of the house, and in front of the truck.

"Terri! Are you crazy?"

"Wait. Stay, I'm sorry. The photo, it's my little brother. His wife and son. I didn't know..." Her eyes filled with tears, and her voice broke. "I couldn't find out what happened to him. They took him away."

Sheila was out of the truck instantly. "Who took him?"

"Child Protective Services. I tried to find him, after I was eighteen and had graduated. I know it sounds bad that I left him. But I had to get away. I was hurt so badly. I told you my art teacher and her boyfriend took me in. The principal and a few other teachers realized what was going on, the abuse…I was afraid I would be sent back. So, I stayed with them for a few months until I graduated and turned eighteen. I went back one day, snuck in the house when everyone was gone. All his stuff was gone. His pictures, clothing, everything. Every trace of Stevie had vanished. I found out he was in a foster home, but they wouldn't let me see him. CPS thought it was in his best interest not to see anyone from his family. I tried, God, I tried, but they wouldn't let me. They assured me he was safe. Eventually I gave up. He disappeared into the system that I was too old for. He was safe and that was all the mattered. Laurie said he came around the school recently trying to find out what happened to me. Apparently, he has tried several times to find me, but no one seemed to know anything. She met with him and told him she knew how to get in touch with me. She gave me his number and address."

"That's good. You can write or call him…Terri, don't you want to get in touch with him?"

Terri paced, pulling her hands through her hair and leaving it in spikes. "What do I say? Hey, I'm your big sister. Sorry I left you to get beaten by our sadistic parents? That I left you alone and defenseless."

"No! Terri, they beat you, hard enough to rip flesh from your back, from your hand. I know from the way your back looks you didn't get medical attention for any of it. You did what you had to do to live. You got away and when you could you went back to find him. The little boy might not have understood, but the man he is now will."

At Terri's continued despair, Sheila pulled Terri into her arms. "Sweetheart, write to him, tell him what you told me. He's looking for you and sent a family picture. He wants to find you. He's wondering if you're okay too. It might bring closure, but maybe it's a beginning, maybe it will let you heal some of the hurt."

"Stay with me. You help me heal every day."

Sheila nodded. "Okay, love. I'll stay the night."

***

Later, Terri lay in bed with Sheila sleeping soundly beside her. She trusted Sheila, more than she had trusted anyone ever before. Trust was a hard thing to give. When the people who were supposed to love you—who were supposed to take care of you—broke that trust, it was a hard thing to risk later.

She trusted Sheila and had come to rely on her for support, and for understanding. The thought of Sheila not being in her life chilled her. She knew what she felt with her was stronger than lust, beyond erotic, and unbelievably powerful. With a sudden jolt, she realized she had fallen in love.

Chapter Twenty-one

SHEILA HAD A VERY busy, productive week at the clinic, and finally felt secure enough with how business was improving that she would not have to reduce staff hours. After meeting with other veterinarians in the region to propose a rotation for emergency coverage, she stopped at a popular restaurant, the Outfitter, for lunch. She had already placed her order at the counter and found a seat when a tall, athletic man approached her table.

"Do you mind if I sit here? I've never seen it so crowded here before."

"Okay." Sheila moved her purse onto the chair's back and pulled her tea in closer.

Sitting down, he extended his hand. "Tim Dugeson. Nice to meet you. Thanks for letting me join you. I hate eating in the car."

"No problem. I'm Sheila McDevitt."

"I don't think I've seen you around before. I would have remembered you." He smiled broadly.

"I moved here about four months ago."

"What do you do?"

"I'm a veterinarian."

"I bet that's interesting."

"It is. I enjoy it very much." Sheila noticed the crisp white shirt and tie. The short haircut and tidy nails. "What do you do?"

"Lawyer. Primarily business law, contract preparation and review."

The waitress brought the food over. Sheila suddenly felt a little self-conscious with the bacon cheeseburger she had ordered. She hesitated for a moment then decided she wasn't trying to impress this man. She added condiments, sliced the burger in half, and took a bite. She stopped herself from groaning as the delicious beef flavor mixed perfectly with the salty taste of the crispy bacon.

"So where is your clinic?"

Sheila wiped her mouth with her napkin. "Over in Bryson City. I took over Dr. James' practice. He had a nice mix of small and large animals, that's what I wanted."

"Where did you study?"

"Texas A&M."

"Oh, the Longhorns."

Sheila nearly choked. "No. The Aggies. Big difference."

He laughed. "I'm curious. Did you keep the contracts with the stables that he had? What I mean is, you didn't do the contract by yourself, did you?"

"It was a standard contract that I've used before."

"Hmm. I could look at it if you want. Before you sign any other contracts, it would be wise to have legal counsel."

"I'll think about it." She sipped her tea and watched as he bit into his meatball sub, obviously being careful to avoid getting the red sauce onto his white shirt. "So, where did you go to school?"

"University of Alabama."

"Oh, the Crimson Tigers." She struggled to keep the smile off her face. Sheila watched as the look of amazement crossed his face, his mouth opening and closing several times before he realized she was joking.

He grinned at her. "That's funny. You had me going for a moment."

"The look on your face was great." She noticed a deep warmth in his brown eyes, a small dimple appeared in his left cheek as he smiled. "So where is your office?"

"I have one up in Cherokee, another down in Franklin. I go up to Cherokee once or twice a week, depending on what's coming up." His watch beeped. "I need to get going. It was very nice meeting you." He reached in his wallet and pulled out a business card, took a few seconds to scribble something on the back. "Here's my card if you want me to review those contracts. Or whatever." His gaze lingered on her.

Sheila smiled accepting the card. "Thank you. It was nice meeting you also."

***

Terri spent a week in the Boundary Waters of Minnesota, photographing for a conservation group. There was primitive camping, beautiful scenery, and stunning nighttime displays from the Aurora Borealis. They traveled by canoe and kayak, portaging when necessary. Black flies swarmed by day, and mosquitoes by night. They were geographically isolated from modern conveniences, including cell coverage, and after seven days Terri was looking forward to returning to North Carolina.

As soon as she returned home, Terri started to download the multitude of images she had taken throughout the week. She took comfort in her usual post trip routine. She cleaned her equipment, recharged batteries, and sorted through her mail. While pulling out her checkbook to pay bills, the picture of her brother and his family fell onto the desk. She sat looking at it, annoyed with the slight shaking of her hand. She reread his letter but did not get any sense of hostility from it. Remembering Sheila's words, she picked up the phone.

"Hello, I'm trying to reach Steven Greene."

"Speaking." His voice was deep and rich.

"This is Terri." She heard his quick intake of breath. "I got your letter."

"God. I can't believe it's you. I've been looking for you. I was hoping you would respond."

"I...I had some traveling to do...for work."

"Yes. Laurie told me. Your art teacher. She said that you're a photographer."

"I am."

"I found your website. It's amazing."

"Thank you." She paused, lost as to what to say. "Umm, ah, how have you been, Stevie?" She walked to a window and looked out at the peaceful scenery.

She heard him sigh. "I didn't think I would ever hear that again."

"Sorry."

"Don't be. You were the only one who ever called me that. It feels great. I'm doing well. I'm married, my wife Marion and I have a little boy, Andy. Another on the way."

"That's great. How long have you been together?"

"Married two years this past March. I never thought I would want to be a parent, but I love it."

She paced across the room. "Congratulations, that's nice. Um, what do you do?"

He hesitated. "Marion and I work with abused children. Counseling and helping them get the assistance they need. Making sure the foster homes are the right one for them."

Terri was speechless for several seconds as memories whipped through her, her stomach tightened, and nausea roiled up. Aware of the growing silence, she whispered, "That's good."

"Terri? Are you all right?"

"Ah, yes." She reached for a chair and collapsed into it before she fell to the floor. "I wasn't expecting that. I don't know what I was expecting. It's good that you can do that. Help them, that way."

"They trust me more knowing that I went through it. I understand the fear, the confusion, and the pain."

Her throat tightened. "Stevie, I'm sorry. I left you. I came back to find you, when I was better." She wiped the tears from her face and shuddered as her stomach seized.

"Stop. Don't cry. I know you tried. They told me you had tried, but they wouldn't let you see me or talk to me. When I found out that's what they did, I was so mad...furious with my foster parents, and CPS, and the whole world. By the time they agreed to let me see you, you had left. No one seemed to know where you were or were willing to say. Where did you go, Terri?"

"I headed south, eventually I got to Virginia. I've been in North Carolina for seven years. I never forgot you, Stevie."

"TT please, stop crying."

Terri's shoulders shuddered with the mention of her brother's childhood nickname for her. She jumped up out of the chair, nearly knocking it over when hands touched lightly on her shoulder. Twisting around she saw Sheila and the look of concern on her face. She wiped at the tears on her face. "I'm sorry. I wasn't expecting to hear from you. To have you want to talk to me, after I left you."

"You didn't leave me. God, Terri, I saw what they did. I lay in bed that night and cried and prayed to God that you got somewhere safe and that you would be okay. I've prayed every night that you were okay and that someday I would find you. I have. When can I see you? I want to see you. I want you to meet my family."

"You want to see me?" She saw Sheila smile, nodding her head as she pulled the calendar from the wall.

"Of course. I have some vacation time coming. I could come down there. What part of North Carolina are you in?"

"The mountains, I'm in Bryson City. It's a long way. We could meet in the middle somewhere."

"Let me talk to Marion. So, are you married?"

"No." At Terri's subtle change of voice and more cautious tone, Sheila looked over to her. "I'm not married. I'm in a relationship but we're...ah..."

"Not there yet." She heard the smile in his voice. "Terri, I hate to cut this short. I've waited so long to talk to you, but I must get going. Can I call you? I'll let you know when and where we can meet."

"Yes. I would like that." She gave him her home and cell numbers.

"I'm so glad you called. Thanks, Terri. I've missed you."

"I've missed you, too. Bye, Stevie."

"Bye, TT."

She hung up the phone, wiped at her eyes, and accepted the tissue from Sheila.

"Are you okay?"

Terri nodded, trying to get her emotions under control. Sheila reached out, stroked her hand along Terri's jaw and lifted her chin. "You called him. That's good. He understood."

"He did. He wants to see me."

"Of course, he does. He's missed you, Terri. When are you going to see him?"

"He's going to find some dates and let me know."

"Maybe Labor Day weekend. Unless you don't want to wait that long."

"Maybe. I missed you." She leaned forward, kissing Sheila gently.

"I missed you, too. I brought over a few groceries. I wasn't sure when you were getting in or if you were coming here or to my place first."

"I had to get started on the download. I was coming over as soon as I had that going but then I—"

Sheila cut her off. "It's okay. I'm glad you called him. Are you hungry?"

"Just for you. Come to bed with me." She nuzzled Sheila's neck, her hands sliding up the back of Sheila's shirt.

Sheila glanced at her watch. "I have to get back shortly. I have an appointment soon."

"I can be fast. Can you?" She released Sheila's bra.

"Let's see."

She was five minutes late.

Chapter Twenty-two

SHEILA WAS INCREASINGLY BUSY at work and found herself often home late and exhausted. She passed on riding with Terri on the bike, and the evening walks with Tripod. She had received several calls from Tim Dugeson that she had yet to return. He was obviously interested in her, and although she had enjoyed lunch with him, she was not interested in pursuing a relationship. *But why do I feel so guilty?*

Sheila was staring out the kitchen window as water ran into the sink one evening, a scowl on her face. With a heavy sigh she slipped her hands into the water to wash the few pans.

"Sheila, what's wrong?" Terri asked.

"Nothing. I'm tired."

"Go sit down. I'll do these. Or better yet, get a shower, I'll give you a massage afterward."

"Thanks." She stroked her hand across Terri's cheek. She leaned forward, but then stopped short of kissing her. "That sounds good. I'll make it up to you."

An hour later, Sheila was sound asleep. The deep massage she had received had put her under quickly. Terri slid into bed next to her, placed a soft kiss on her shoulder before she fell asleep. She slept restlessly and, in the morning vague memories of a dream where someone stood off to the side watching her flitted away as soon as she awakened fully.

***

Terri stopped by the clinic at lunch time to visit.

Becky greeted Terri. "Hey, Terri, how are you doing? How was Minnesota?"

"Beautiful. I was up in the boundary waters. Bugs were crazy, but other than that it was a good trip."

"Sheila should be finished soon, she's doing a surgery. You can go back to her office and wait if you like. That food smells great."

Terri started to set out the food she had brought, and while pouring two glasses of sweet tea knocked one over. It ran down the front of the desk and into a partially opened drawer. Grabbing the napkins, she blotted up the spill. She opened the drawer and saw pooled tea in there also. She ran out to the restroom and got more paper towels to clean up the mess. Removing items from the drawer, she found a business card. Tim Dugeson. *God, please don't let Sheila be considering him for her lawyer. Relatively good-looking, for a guy, a sharp dresser, he chased women all over the tri-county area.*

He was an average lawyer at best. He had pursued Terri enthusiastically despite her multiple rejections and remained persistent until she and Jackson had gone on several mutually beneficial 'dates.' Flipping over the card she saw his home number handwritten on the back. Her stomach gave a little flip. She discarded the wet paper towels, wiped the drawer out with clean wet towels and placed everything dry back in. Sheila came in while Terri was sorting through the wet papers. Terri saw the smile freeze on Sheila's face.

"What are you doing?"

"I spilled tea. It went down into the drawer. I got it cleaned up but there are some wet papers. I'm sorry."

Sheila came over, looked down at the papers, and glanced through them. "They're nothing important." She took them from Terri and tossed them in the trash can. She ran her fingers through the drawer ensuring it was not sticky before sliding it closed. She missed Terri's frown. "I wasn't expecting you."

"I thought I would surprise you."

"You did." Sheila glanced at the door, walked over and closed it. She smiled slightly. "It is a nice surprise."

Not entirely convinced, Terri leaned over and kissed her softly. "Are you sure?"

"Sure, of what?"

"That this was a nice surprise."

Sheila pulled back. "Of course, it is. Why would you ask that?" She walked behind the desk, pulled her chair back toward the desk. "I wasn't expecting to find you here going through my desk."

"I wasn't going through your desk. I spilled tea. I was cleaning it up."

"I know that," Sheila snapped. With a huff she sat down in the chair. "Shit!" Jumping up she held her hands to her butt, now wet from the spilled drink. "Goddamn it."

"Sorry. I didn't realize it got on the chair. Do you have anything to change into?"

"Yes. I have more scrubs in the back." She walked out of her office, ignoring the glances from Becky and Jamie. She returned several minutes later. Terri had brought in chairs from the lunchroom and had set sandwiches onto plates as well as fresh fruit salad. As Sheila sat down, Terri apologized again.

"It's okay. Stop apologizing. It's not a big deal," Sheila said tightly.

"It shouldn't be."

Sheila looked up, her eyes glinted. "What are you saying?"

"Nothing. Forget it." Terri shook her head slightly from side to side. "Please, can you take a few minutes and eat before you have to start again."

Sheila picked up the sandwich and started eating. They ate in silence, the air frosty between them. As they were finishing there was a knock on the door. Sheila called out and the door opened.

"Doc, someone just brought in a dog hit by a car. It's pregnant, and it doesn't look good." Jamie hurried down the hall as Sheila raced out of the room.

Terri cleaned up from lunch, wrapped the remaining half sandwich, and placed it in the fridge in the little lunchroom. She scribbled a note to Sheila and left it on her desk and gave a silent wave to Becky, who was trying to get information from a very distraught client as she left.

***

Terri finished her work out on the Bowflex, and then went for a run. The pounding of her feet on the trail was soothing and helped clear her head so she could settle down. She was more upset than she cared to admit. Something had been off since she got back from her trip. Unable to pinpoint it, she continued her run, focusing on the trail in front of her.

An hour later she was throwing a ball with Tripod and recalled finding Dugeson's business card. If he was trying to get Sheila as a client she needed to discourage that. He was not well respected. His home number on the back of the card was concerning. But if she said anything to Sheila about the card, Sheila would think she was rooting through her desk. She decided to not to mention it unless Sheila brought it up.

***

Sheila came out of her office to give charts to Becky and noticed flowers on the counter. "Those are pretty."

"They were brought in for you," Becky replied.

"Me?"

"Tim Dugeson brought them by. I told him you were in surgery, so he didn't stick around."

She looked at the flowers and back at Jamie and Becky. She noticed the curious looks on their faces. "Those are nice. I think I'll leave them out here, so everyone can enjoy them." She walked away without ever touching the flowers.

Leaving the office an hour later, the fragrance of the flowers wafted on the air as she walked by. She stopped and looked at them, a feeling of unease coming over her. She turned away, set the alarm, and locked up. When she got home, she was surprised not to see Terri's Jeep, and with a deep sigh, she realized she was relieved. She needed time to unwind and to figure out why Terri's visit had upset her.

Sheila finished an hour of yoga and felt more relaxed than she had in several days. She showered and sat down to read, getting up several minutes later to get something to eat. She stood staring in front of the open refrigerator and realized this was the first time in several months that she hadn't had dinner with Terri if she was in town. Sitting down for dinner she felt strangely alone in the quiet house.

She picked at her salad while the clock ticked impossibly loud. *Why did I get so mad at her? She was trying to clean up the tea. But why did it bother me so much that she was in my desk? And those flowers. God, I am going to have to call Dugeson to tell him I'm not interested.*

Giving up with eating her dinner she placed it in the refrigerator for lunch the next day. Leaning back against the counter she realized what had bothered her. *His card was in the drawer. He's attractive, and interesting to talk to. It's not like I cheated. Did I? I need to apologize.* She glanced at the clock, grabbed her keys and left.

***

The house was dark as she pulled up into the driveway. Tripod stood barking, and then whining, her tail wagging vigorously as Sheila emerged from the truck.

"Hi there, Tripod. How are you?" She rubbed the dog's neck and behind its ears as she looked around. A small glow from the kitchen window was the only light visible inside.

Terri's Jeep was there so Sheila walked to the shed to see if the bike was inside. The lock was released. Sheila opened the door and saw the glow of the bike's reflector in the darkness of the shed. Closing the door, she turned and let out a shriek as Terri stood in front of her. She clutched her hand to her chest as her heart thudded.

"Damn, you scared me. Don't you ever make any noise when you walk?" Sheila saw the furrow of Terri's brow, and the carefully blank look on her face. Her brown eyes looked flat and sad.

"Terri, I'm sorry about earlier today. I acted poorly." Reaching out, she stroked her hand against Terri's jaw, and was surprised when it tensed, and Terri pulled away. "Terri, please, I'm sorry."

Terri looked Sheila in the eyes and rubbed at her own eyebrows. "It was a rough day for everyone. How's the dog?"

Confused, Sheila looked at Tripod. "The dog?"

"Yes, at the clinic."

"Oh, well, four of the pups are alive. The rest of the litter and the mom didn't make it. They'll have to be bottle fed."

"Are you all right?"

"Yes. It's not the first time and it won't be the last. The family has a lot of work cut out for them." She swatted at a mosquito. "Can we go inside and talk?"

Terri locked the shed and they went inside. "Would you like something to drink?"

"Whatever you're having."

Terri filled two large glasses with ice water added a slice of lemon and handed one to Sheila. Gesturing to the table, she sat down. "What's going on, Sheila?"

An awkward silence followed. *It shouldn't be so hard, talking after a little misunderstanding.* "I had a bad day and I didn't know you were coming by. I was surprised to find you, and then, well, you were rooting through my desk."

"I was cleaning up—"

"I know. I realize that. I didn't think, Terri. It came out wrong."

"Do I need to call before I come over?"

"No. Terri, it was a nice surprise. I blew it. Not you. Please forgive me."

"I do." Terri smiled. "I missed talking to you at dinner. And Tripod thought she was going to starve without the little scraps you sneak her."

"It's just vegetables."

"Mmm hmm. Sure, it is."

Sheila laughed and pulled Terri over to her, and their eyes met. Sheila started to lean in then stopped, searching Terri's face. "Kiss me, Terri."

***

Terri brushed her hands along Sheila's cheeks, lowered her lips to Sheila's, but the kiss was light and didn't linger. She leaned back and reached for her glass. She took a long drink of water as her thoughts raced. *Ask her about the business card.*

Sheila stood, walked around to Terri and pulled her close. "Kiss me again. Like you mean it this time. Take me to bed."

With the niggling image of a business card in her head, and Sheila with the handsome lawyer, Terri fisted her hands in Sheila's hair, crushing their mouths together. White-hot heat raced through her, consuming her body as her mind blanked except for possessing Sheila, taking her, making her forget about that man.

Her hands flew over Sheila, pulling at her blouse quickly, yanking it up and over her head before tossing it on the floor. Pressing Sheila against the wall, she pushed her thigh between Sheila's legs, spreading her legs, as her mouth plundered. Pulling her mouth away, her own breathing labored, she tugged urgently at Sheila's pants, forcing them down as Sheila fumbled to release her own bra.

She pushed Sheila's hands away, ripping the bra from her. Lifting Sheila, muscles straining slightly, she walked to the bedroom, her teeth nipping at Sheila's collarbone, not afraid of marking her. Falling onto the bed with Sheila, she yanked her pants off the rest of the way. She jerked Sheila down to her by the hips, lifted Sheila's legs, placing them over her shoulders, lowered her mouth and feasted.

***

Sheila was surprised, aroused and overwhelmed at Terri's quick sexual aggression. She tried to keep up, to get some control, but was swept along in a torrent of sensation. She gasped and struggled, trying to reach up, to pull Terri to her, but her hips were jerked higher, forcing more of her own weight onto her shoulders, exposing her more to Terri's wicked mouth. With her breath backing up in her lungs and consuming heat racing through her body, she grasped at the sheets to hold on.

Terri nibbled on her outer lips as she arched violently and started to spasm. As her clit was pulled into the warm moist mouth and lashed with soft flicks of tongue, she erupted, shouting out incomprehensible sounds as she surrendered to pleasure.

Sheila lay motionless on the bed except for the rapid rise and fall of her chest. She looked in stunned wonderment as she watched Terri stand up and undress, tugging her own clothes off. Her breath caught in her chest as she heard Terri say, "I hope you're ready, we're not done yet."

Roslyn Bane

Chapter Twenty-three

TERRI AWAKENED WITH A jerk, the dream instantly fading, leaving behind an uneasy feeling. She rolled onto her side, leaning on her elbow. Sheila was sleeping, her blonde hair tousled and spread across the pillow, her lower lip slightly swollen. Terri reached out to sweep hair from Sheila's face, but flinched when she saw the marks on Sheila's collarbone, and on her breasts. *God, what did I do?* Backing away, Terri pressed a hand to her stomach as bile rose in her throat.

Sheila pulled her back down. "Where do you think you're going?"

"I hurt you."

Sheila sat up, looked at her breasts, her hips, and saw the bruising. "No, you didn't."

"I bruised you. I hurt you."

Sheila reached out and grabbed Terri's hand before she could flee. "So what, you bruised me. You didn't hurt me, I didn't break. We had rough, energetic sex. Very enjoyable sex. The only way it could have been better was if you would've smacked me on the ass once or twice right before I came."

Terri couldn't stop the recoil as she jerked, just as she couldn't stop the blood rushing from her face. She fell back onto her ass, sitting on the bed, her hand rubbing at her chest as a million thoughts ran through her head. "You want me to hit you?"

She tried to stand up, but was jerked back down, clutching at air as she was flipped onto her back. She tried to push up and was quickly pinned as Sheila settled across her pelvis, holding her arms down at her sides.

"Yes. No. Listen to me. Not in anger, not in desperation, not in some mistaken belief that someone deserves to be hit. But I like getting a swat across my ass, right as I get close. Not all the time. Just every now and then, a surprise."

Head shaking vigorously, "I couldn't. No. Absolutely not."

Sheila leaned forward and ran a finger over Terri's lips. "Okay. Sex is supposed to be fun, to be enjoyable. I've had fun every time with you,

Terri. I also liked what we did last night." She gave a little groan as Terri looked away. "Terri, look at me." She waited until Terri looked right at her. "You didn't hurt me. You would never hurt me."

Terri said nothing. Sheila stood and pulled Terri up by the hand. She placed her hands on Terri's cheeks, cradling her. "I need you to understand that you did not hurt me." Terri sat in silence. "Terri, talk to me. Do you understand what I am saying to you?"

Terri saw the concern on Sheila's face. It warred with the bruises she could see and the violent memories of her past. After a few seconds she pursed her lips. "I don't get it, but I understand." She stood and started to walk away. "I'm starving. Do you want an omelet or pancakes? I'm cooking."

***

August arrived in torrents of rain, as tropical depressions drifted up from the Texas Gulf Coast and stalled over the mountains. Terri traveled into Charlotte staying a few days to shoot several ad campaigns while the weather was foul.

She worked out in the hotel gym, sometimes twice daily, and during those times her mind drifted to Sheila and their sex life. Things had changed, no matter what Sheila said. It didn't matter how much Sheila tried to reassure Terri that their sex life was as good as always, Terri felt she was letting her lover down. The thought of striking her for enjoyment was a foreign and a terrifying thought, and it grew into a deep dark threat in dreams that had returned with increasing frequency and violence.

***

Sheila couldn't stand being inside anymore, she pulled on her raincoat, jumped into her truck and went driving. An hour later she pulled into the Outfitter for lunch, ordering a trout cake sandwich, onion rings, and sweet tea. She was halfway through her lunch and browsing through the local paper when she was interrupted.

"Hi, there. It's nice to see you again."

"Well, hi." She smiled at Tim, but inwardly she groaned. The guy was persistent. Becky and Jamie had warned her of his reputation. She had also mentioned his name in passing to Terri, who had looked strangely uncomfortable as she had answered that Sheila could find a much better lawyer to handle her business than him.

Tim slid a chair out, sitting across from Sheila. With a mental sigh she closed the paper, folded it and placed it under her purse. Brought up to be respectful and polite, she spent thirty minutes engaged in conversation. Much to her chagrin, she found his conversation interesting and witty. The man had an interesting outlook on several major social-political issues, and he had a wicked sense of humor. Their lunch was interrupted when she received a call saying that she was needed at the clinic.

As she drove away, she began to feel uncomfortable, just as she had the last time, she had lunch with him. She now recognized it as guilt. She knew instinctively not to mention lunch with him to Terri. Their relationship had been strained since she had suggested to Terri to smack her ass.

With a silent swear she asked herself for the millionth time how she could have been so stupid to have asked an abused person to strike her. She had tried to reassure Terri that it wasn't necessary, but Sheila felt her lover struggle as she battled her inner demons and her desire to please her partner. And as her own guilt grew, she found herself withdrawing, not daring to kiss or hug Terri for fear of putting her under more pressure.

Chapter Twenty-four

SHEILA PACED AROUND HER home office, phone pressed to her ear. "Peter, I am not going up to Virginia to hobnob with a bunch of people who aren't part of my life anymore."

"We always went to it and had a great time."

"You had a good time. I was the good little wife, an ornament on your arm."

"Do me this favor, please."

She laughed out loud. "You have some nerve. Take your secretary. Peter, it's not like everyone doesn't know that we're divorced, and you were banging her. Why are you even trying to go to this event? Aren't the bright lights of Los Angeles shiny enough for you?"

"Damn it, just come. I need you there," Peter said with irritation.

"You need an image there." Pulling gently at her hair she stood and stared out the window. "I'm not going with anyone. Listen to me."

Peter interrupted her. "I can find someone to escort you. We can both attend and at least be civil to each other. Show people we parted on good terms."

She was momentarily speechless with the audacity of his statement. "Listen to me. I. Am. Not. Going. With. Anyone."

"You're being stubborn. You're still hurting. By God, Sheila, you still love me."

"Love? That will be a cold day in hell," Sheila shouted. "For the last time, Peter, I am not going with anyone. Sign the damn papers for the house sale, Peter. We won't get a better offer. Then you can buy your little princess whatever the hell she wants." Sheila slammed the phone down. "Goddamn it! What a bastard!" She turned and saw Terri in the doorway. "Sorry, that was Peter. God, he pisses me off. He needs to sign the papers and the house is sold. I can't believe…" She trailed off at the look on Terri's face. "Terri? What's wrong?"

"Did you mean that? What you said?" Terri's voice hitched.

"What? The phone call? Of course, I did."

Terri's face paled, and her eyes went flat. She turned and hurried away before turning back to face Sheila. "I see. Well that explains some things." She picked up her bag and keys, striding to the side door.

Sheila scrambled after her. "Terri? What's going on?"

"What's going on? You tell me! I heard you! You're not going with anyone? I guess that explains why lately this relationship, no, whatever this is, feels so one-sided. Only one of us is invested."

"What are you talking about?" Sheila pleaded.

"You. Now I get it. Now, finally, I get why you don't make the first move. Not to call me, not to kiss me, certainly not to make love with me."

Sheila rushed toward her. "Terri, I don't know what—" She was interrupted by the doorbell. "Shit!" Sheila answered the front door and was surprised by the flower delivery. Sniffing them she turned back into the room, and looked up in time to see hurt, then anger on Terri's face. She hurried over to place them on the kitchen counter. "Terri, I'm not sure what's—"

"Who are they from?"

"I don't know." She didn't want to open the card. Not now. She wasn't sure what was going on, and opening the card wasn't going to improve the situation. "Terri?"

"Open it!" Terri demanded.

Hands trembling Sheila opened the card. "They're from Tim Dugeson, he—"

Terri grabbed the card. "I enjoyed lunch, looking forward to getting to know you better." Terri tossed the card on the counter and stormed outside. "Tripod! Come!" The dog wheeled over. Terri unhooked the wheelchair, scooped Tripod up and placed her gently in the Jeep. She picked up the harness and collapsed it down.

"Terri, what's wrong? Talk to me."

Slamming the tailgate, she whipped around. "You think I'm a fool? Have you had a good time experimenting with your little lesbian friend? To hell with you."

Sheila stood alone and confused in the driveway as Terri jumped in the Jeep and roared away. After standing stunned for several minutes she ran into the house and grabbed her purse and keys. Running back out she pulled up short and watched her parents pull into her driveway.

***

Terri raced into her driveway, sliding to a stop. With tears blurring her vision, she stumbled out of the Jeep, opened the tailgate and tried to lift Tripod down. The dog whined and licked at her face. She wiped at her tears.

"Stop, Tripod." She lifted the dog down, brought the wheelchair out and walked to the house. Entering, she looked around as if seeing it for the first time. The bright colors appeared in stark contrast to the woodwork. Garish. The furniture now lumbered, an oversized monstrosity for a single person. She looked at Tripod. "Why do you stay with me? Why do you even like me?" The dog whined and nudged at her leg. With the echoes of her parents berating her, she went to the refrigerator and pulled out a beer. She guzzled it down, took the time to feed and water the dog, and grabbed another beer.

She changed clothes quickly and went upstairs. Turning on the iPod, she cranked up the volume, increased the resistance on the Bowflex, and started lifting. Muscles straining with the increased weight, she worked out. Her hands blistered.

She overwhelmed her body with pain as she fought to drown out her emotions. She drank while she exercised. Finishing the grueling session, she hurried downstairs, and went outside with the dog. Engulfed in the darkness, the thick humid air clogged her lungs and she felt utterly alone.

Tripod returned, and the dog stood watching as Terri grabbed another beer and a bottle of whiskey and went back upstairs. She lowered the volume and switched to dark and broody classical music. As the first strains of Toccata and Fugue in D minor filled the room, she fought back tears.

Staring out the window into the darkness, she opened the whiskey bottle and drank heavily. Plopping onto the chaise lounge, her hands fisted as she struggled with the humiliation she felt, with the silent desperation of knowing her parents were right.

Her fingers pressed into the fresh blisters until she bled, unnoticed. She opened the beer, studied the label and downed it in several long swallows. Her gaze fell on the charcoal drawings. She stalked over, looked at them, and in a moment of rage, tore them from the wall, throwing them across the room. She yanked a pad from the rack, pulled out her charcoal and sketched, her fingers flying over paper.

She poured herself into the drawings and smudged them with blood. When she finished, she pulled the paper from the pad, pushing it to the floor. Half staggering to the window, she looked out, picked up the bottle of whiskey, and drank. Vivaldi's Summer filled the air as she returned to the table and set the bottle aside. With tears coursing down her face she drew, filling page after page, discarding them on the floor. Finally, exhausted, she stumbled down the stairs, and fell across the bed.

***

Warm moist air heralded the coming storm and thunder pounded. Terri awakened and groaned. It took her several long moments to realize the thunder was her own skull pounding. The warm moist air, dog breath. As soon as she opened her eyes, Tripod whined, licked at her face and her hand as she tried to shield herself. She rolled over, every muscle in her body aching. Tripod crawled onto the bed and lay against Terri, her muzzle resting on Terri's chest. Terri stroked the dog, trying to wish her headache away.

She had to pee, but was afraid to get up, knowing that her head would explode. When she could wait no longer, she got up, steadied herself, and took two steps before the first wave of nausea hit. She ran to the bathroom, bumping into the dresser, knocking pictures over, before bouncing off the doorframe, her elbow taking the blow. She made it to the bathroom, falling to her knees before vomiting fiercely.

She finished and crawled to the tub, turned on the faucet and stuck her head under it. The cold water was biting, cooling her sweat-soaked body as she let the water flow until she shivered. Turning off the tap, she grabbed a towel, tried to dry her hair, and finally gave up. She emptied her bladder, and after two attempts to stand she pulled herself up to the counter, looked at her reflection for a moment before slamming her hand against the mirror, breaking it. Tripod watched and whimpered, her ears pulled back low. "What do you want?" The dog only watched and waited.

Another wave of nausea hit Terri as she turned. She heaved repeatedly into the bowl until it felt as if her insides had ripped free. She curled into a ball on the floor, shaking fiercely and felt Tripod curl up next to her.

Terri awakened several hours later. Tripod stood immediately and barked at her. "Shh, you're too loud." Terri looked at the broken mirror, carefully opening the medicine cabinet and pulled out the aspirin. She fumbled with the bottle, swearing until she got the lid off, and took two with some water. "I bet you need to go out." Tripod barked and scrambled to the door.

Walking outside, Terri shielded her eyes from the glare of the high sun and she realized it was midafternoon. She moved back indoors and refilled the dog bowls before setting them on the porch. She went to the kitchen, filled a huge glass with water, and drank it immediately. Returning to the bathroom, she stripped and stepped cautiously into the shower, allowing the brisk water to gradually warm.

She showered, the smell of the shampoo almost overpowering. She gagged, but with nothing left to come out she suffered through dry heaves. Finally, she emerged from the shower and pulled on sweatpants and a T-shirt. She checked on Tripod who was lazing in the sun, then nibbled at some crackers and sipped at some water. She thought she might feel human in another day.

Setting the glass in the sink she noticed the message light was blinking. She started to walk away but routine had her turning back to retrieve the messages. An unfamiliar voice filled the room. Was she interested in traveling to British Columbia to do photos for an American travel magazine? The caller provided the callback number and asked Terri to please call by four o'clock. Terri glanced at the clock, it was three fifty-five.

Grabbing the phone, Terri called immediately. For the next twenty minutes the details of the trip were explained. The scheduled photographer had been hurt and was unable to fulfill the contract and had recommended Terri. The shoot was to start in two days. Terri knew her schedule was light and thought that the time away would help her heal her emotional wounds. Reimbursement and expenses were discussed and agreed upon. Terri went upstairs and waited for the faxed copy of the contract to arrive. She reviewed it carefully, called her lawyer, explained the urgency of the situation and faxed it to her for review.

While she waited, she looked about the room. She didn't have time to clean up. She moved to the locked closets, punched in the digital codes to release the locks and opened the heavy doors. Looking over the selection of cameras and lenses, she selected her equipment, packing it in protective cases. She checked her batteries, took backups and rechargers. Moving to her desk she retrieved several memory cards, then loaded them into her computer to ensure they were empty and ready. She loaded all but one into a protective case. She went back to the closet and stared at the first camera she owned, reaching for it. She checked it, ensuring it functioned well, then slid the memory card in and packed the camera in a soft-sided case that would fit in her carry-on.

She checked the weather at her destination, pulled up files she had previously made and printed off a packing list. She shut down her computer, grabbed her laptop and portable battery and packed that into her carry-on. By the time she was finished packing her clothes, her lawyer had called back, making her recommendations. Terri signed the contract and faxed it back to the client.

She finally went outside, greeted Tripod enthusiastically and put the harness on her. Attaching the leash, they set off for a long walk. An hour later they returned. Terri cooked a relatively bland dinner, which she shared with Tripod. Glancing at the clock, she considered if she left tonight for the airport, she would get a decent night's sleep and have time to ensure the proper instructions for handling her equipment. She knew Jamie was scheduled to work late and called the clinic to find out if she could drop Tripod off tonight. An hour later she was heading out of town, the dog safe at the clinic.

Chapter Twenty-five

SHEILA ARRIVED EARLY THE next morning, greeted her staff, and informed them that her parents were in town and would be stopping by later. For now, she was pleased to have some time without her parents. She had tried several times to call Terri, but the calls went unanswered and she didn't leave messages. She was hurt by the things Terri had said. She recognized that somehow, she had hurt Terri also, but was at a loss of what it was. Her parents had cautiously probed, trying to find out what had Sheila subdued and edgy but had finally given up.

"Was this visit from your parents expected?" Jamie asked.

"No, it was a surprise. They're going on a short rafting trip today and are looking forward to it. Who is first on the schedule today?" She paused and looked toward the back when she heard a familiar bark. "Is Tripod back there?"

"Yes. Terri brought her in last night, right before close. She booked her for two weeks."

"Two weeks?"

"Something came up quick for her. She paid in advance. She asked me not to call you. I tried anyway, to let you know, but there was no answer. Since it wasn't an emergency, I didn't leave a message. I know you don't like leaving her here overnight."

"No, it's all right. Do you know where she went?"

"Somewhere in Canada. You know what was strange, though? She didn't seem excited about the trip and she looked ill."

"She was sick? What do you mean?"

"She was pale, dark circles under her eyes and she sounded stuffy. No makeup. I mean, she doesn't wear a lot, but there was none. She was deathly pale. Is everything okay?"

"I'm not sure. We had a disagreement. Since my parents have been here, we haven't had a chance to talk."

Frowning, Sheila walked into the back to greet the hysterically barking dog and wondered where Terri was traveling to. She hoped she wouldn't be doing anything dangerous. With a sudden jolt she wondered if Terri was going to swing over to New York to see her brother. As much as she wanted Terri to meet him, she wanted to be with Terri to offer support when they finally met again.

That evening Sheila and Tripod went to Terri's. Sheila gathered up Tripod's medicine, and a few toys. Noticing a beer bottle on an end table she picked it up, rinsed it and went to place it in the recycle bin. Passing the bathroom, she noticed the light left on. She glanced in and stood shocked at the broken mirror, still somehow in the frame. "Oh my God! What the hell?"

Feeling a rock in the pit of her stomach, and tension creep up the back of her neck, she moved quickly to the bedroom and looked around. She rearranged the knocked over pictures and straightened the bed. Looking at the pillow, she picked it up and studied it, smudges of reddish brown and gray on the normally spotless linen. Realization dawned that it was blood. She wandered around trying to find what Terri may have cut herself on. The mirror in the bath was broken but had not fallen, so something else must have caused the blood. Tripod barked and started up the stairs, so Sheila followed.

The dog entered the room and whined. "Tripod, no, you shouldn't be—" She stopped, and stared. "Oh my God." Glancing at the framed pictures on the floor she turned and glanced at the empty wall. "Oh no." She hurried over and picked up the drawings. The frames were cracked, there was a slight tear in one, but otherwise they seemed undamaged. She placed them on the work counter and closed the nearly empty bottle of whiskey.

She started picking up the papers on the floor, then stopped and looked at one. Dropping to her knees, her hand at her throat, tears sprang to her eyes. Dark and moody did not come close to describing the drawing. This was despair. She knew the figure in the picture, recognized it immediately, and knew the reddish-brown smudge on the page was blood.

She spread out the other sketches, a small child surrounded by impossibly tall adults, the child clearly injured while smiling adults stood by disinterested. Another held a group of couples with a lone figure off to the side watching them. The other took longer to identify but caused Sheila to shiver. A window with each pane filled with a violent scene; death, anger, lightning, and sickness. "God, Terri! What were you thinking? What are you doing?"

Sweat sheened on her, and her heart thudded. A wave of nausea rose up. Spreading the drawings on the work surface, her throat tight, she stroked her finger along them and said a silent prayer for Terri. She started gathering up the empty beer bottles and whiskey. As she turned to the leave the room, she noticed the unlocked closets. She had never asked Terri what was in them and had never seen them unlocked. She stood looking at them, and curiosity got the better of her. She slid the door open further. A variety of lenses, filters, and camera gear was carefully arranged on shelves. Empty spaces in between marked removed equipment. Guessing at the value of the remaining gear, she closed the door and pushed the lock symbol. She listened as the lock set.

She turned her attention to the other closet and stood in shock. A handgun, shotgun, rifle, nunchuks, and a baton sat on the shelves. Folded neatly were several rows of belts, a rainbow of colors. She recognized them as the belts received in martial arts. She picked up the neatly stacked papers, looked through them and saw that Terri had black belts in both judo and karate. "Wow, learned to protect yourself, didn't you?"

A few photos of Terri at what must have been her high school graduation with a Chinese couple and what must have been some of her teachers. "God, they didn't even come to your graduation." She swiped at the tears that were forming. "How do you carry that kind of pain, Terri?" Replacing everything carefully, she closed and locked the cabinet.

Gathering the bottles, she called to Tripod, and watched as the dog slid down the steps. After placing the bottles in the recycle bin, she took a last glance around, making sure everything was in order. She picked up the gear she needed for Tripod, secured the house and drove home.

***

Tripod barked as they entered her home. Growling, teeth bared, she stood in front of Sheila, shielding her from the two people in her kitchen. Everyone froze as the dog stood alert and tense. "It's okay, Tripod. Sit." The dog sat immediately. Sheila ruffled her head before walking over to her parents. "She's all right. She's very protective." She hugged her parents. "Come, Tripod."

"She has three legs," her mother exclaimed.

"Yes. She was hit by a car." Sheila stood by as her parents greeted the dog, whose thumping tail soon broke the tension.

"Is this a client's dog?" her father asked.

"Well. Yes."

"Honey? Do you think it wise to bring a client's dog to your home? What if she got loose, and got hurt?"

"It's okay, Mom. Tripod belongs to a friend. She's going to stay here for a few days. Her owner's out of town for a while."

"Her owner? That's a strange way of referring to a friend. What's your friend's name?"

"Terri. Terri Greene."

"The photographer?" At Sheila's look of surprise her father spoke, pointing to the magazine sitting on the coffee table. "I read the article. I was wondering why you had a professional photography magazine."

"Yes. We're friends. Tripod was a stray. Unfortunately, or maybe fortunately, she was hit by Terri. Instead of leaving the poor thing in the road to die she picked her up and brought her to me. I couldn't save her leg, but as you can see, she is a wonderful dog."

"And very protective of you." They watched as the dog nudged at a closet. Sheila walked over, opened the closet and handed her a dog biscuit. The dog flopped down and munched happily. "It seems like she knows her way around."

"Yes, she's here a couple nights a week." Sheila stopped talking and dragged her teeth across her bottom lip. *Shit.* Trying to cover the slip, she changed topics. "Would you like something to drink? Tell me about your rafting trip."

Her mom stepped over, placing her hand on Sheila's. "What's going on, Sheila? You've been a little tense since we got here. We thought at first that it was because the business wasn't going well, but it's something more. Something else is wrong."

"Business is picking up. It's not out of the woods yet. But it's okay." Sheila uncorked a bottle of wine, poured hastily into three glasses, sloshing a little onto the counter.

"Sheila." The tone in her father's voice had her looking up, suddenly feeling like a scared teenager again.

Sheila gazed at her parents and knew she had to decide now what to tell them. She handed them their wine. "Come sit down, I want to tell you something."

Her parents sat on the sofa, Sheila across from them in a chair. Tripod padded over, then sat, leaning into Sheila, who patted her head and drank half of her wine. "I, well...Terri and I are...um, well." She pulled at her collar, her heart thundering in her chest "Well, we're friends. Umm. Very good friends." At her parents' blank stares, she elaborated. "We're lovers." She closed her eyes on her mother's quick intake of breath, reopened them when her father shifted on the couch. The silence grew. Tripod nuzzled at her hand. She finished her wine.

"I know you weren't expecting this. Before, I know you thought it was a phase I was going through. But it's not. I am bisexual. I always have been."

"Is that why your marriage broke up?" her mother asked.

"No! Peter cheated. I never did. I was faithful to him from the moment we started dating."

"Honey, don't you think maybe you've rushed into this because you're hurting?"

"No, Mom. Listen, I didn't expect this. I certainly wasn't looking for a relationship when I moved down here. Not with anyone. But Terri is special. The way she makes me feel is, well...extraordinary." She looked at her father. "I know you're disappointed."

"No. I'm worried. You're not living in a city where this is more accepted, but out here in a small town. You were unhappy with Peter. I would have been disappointed if you would have given up on your dream completely and stayed with him out of convenience." He was holding her mother's hand.

"We want you happy and safe, dear."

"I am."

"So, are we going to meet Terri?"

"Not this trip." At the looks of disappointment, she explained. "She's out of town. She dropped off Tripod at the kennel last night. A job came up suddenly and she left."

Her father asked, "She didn't call you?"

"Um. Well normally she would have, but we had a disagreement. It was right before you got here. I haven't had a chance to talk to her since. A job came up and she had to leave. I went by her place and picked up some of Tripod's things. Anyhow, her flight plans were on the counter, she should be in Canada by now."

Her parents looked at each other before her father spoke. "Sheila, is this relationship healthy? If she gets mad, won't talk, and then storms away?"

"No, it's not like that. Terri is very even tempered. But she hates conflict. She would rather fall back, regroup, and then address things. It's not done to be mean. It's protective."

"Protective?"

"She had a very rough childhood...she would hate that I am sharing this. She was abused, physically and verbally, throughout her life. When her parents found out she was a lesbian they beat her severely. She left home after that. She finished high school and has done very well for herself. I've never felt she did anything out of meanness or spite."

"But you're hurting, too."

"I wish I could figure out what I did to hurt her. She came in when I was on the phone with Peter. He won't sign the papers on the house sale. He thinks we can get more for it but it's the best offer we've had. Then he said he would sign if I went to that charity event for the hospital we always went to. He wants me to come with him or one of his friends. I told him I wasn't going with anyone and I...oh my God." She jumped up to pace, ran her hands across her mouth. "Oh God! That's it. Damn it."

"Sheila?" Her mother rose and came to her, placing a hand on her shoulder.

"She heard me tell Peter I wasn't going with anyone. He said I was only mad because I still loved him. I meant that I wasn't going to that damn fundraiser, she thinks I denied our relationship, or that it isn't important to me."

"But why would she think that?"

"Her parents. They were monsters. They had her convinced she was unlovable, worthless. You can't begin to understand. Sometimes I don't. Terri is so strong, so sure of herself and at odd times her vulnerability comes out, and she's this scared abused kid, trapped in an adult body, afraid to get hurt again."

"Has she gotten help? To deal with it? The after-effects?"

"We've talked about it. It's hard. I think maybe she will, but then she backs down. She has to want to get it for herself, not because I've asked her to."

"What are you going to do now?"

She looked at her parents. "Convince her of the truth. I love her."

Chapter Twenty-six

OVER THE NEXT FEW weeks, Terri worked tirelessly. She photographed the adventures and adventurers she traveled with. Photographed the guides working with the clients. She hiked steep mountains, rappelled, rafted, kayaked, and rode horses until her legs and ass were chaffed. She conversed freely with her companions and enjoyed time around the campfire in the evenings. Some nights, long after the fires had died, she went out to capture the night sky, and the northern lights.

Staying busy helped Terri bury the pain, but at night as she settled for the evening, she struggled. Caught between anger and anguish she heard Sheila's comments. 'I am not going with anyone.' She saw the flowers delivered and Sheila's deep smile of appreciation. She remembered the countless times she waited for Sheila to return from work, so she could spend time with her, cook for her. *Lovesick fool. Waiting for attention like a puppy. Waiting on Sheila like my mother did for my miserable father.*

Whenever she slept, she relived beatings, harsh words, being forced to watch as her father beat her dog to death in a violent outburst before turning on her and her little brother. *How could I be so stupid to have fallen for someone like Sheila? She is so far out of my league, country clubs, fancy homes, and frequent overseas travel. Texas A&M. I have a high school diploma and a community college degree. For God sake, I've been homeless. Lived under bridges and in dark alleys for months. What would Sheila think about that? Or that I have had to fight to defend myself several times. Too bad I couldn't defend my heart this time. Stupid, stupid, stupid. I thought I found someone. She fooled me. I thought she listened. I thought she cared.*

Terri burrowed down into the bed, tossed and turned before finally pulling the spare pillow close and wrapping her arms around it. She sighed, mentally kicking herself. *Snap out of it. Go home and face Sheila, tell her you need to keep the contract going. Drop off Tripod when Sheila is not at the clinic. That will help. Until some time has passed. Damn it! All I wanted was honesty. She should have told me she wanted out of the relationship. Why does this hurt more than anything else ever has? Keep working. Pick up another contract. Move on. Okay. Let's get back, get going and move forward.*

***

Terri knocked several times on the door and after several seconds rang the doorbell. She paced across the front stoop and rang again as Tripod barked. "Hey, Tripod, what are you doing in there? Are you by yourself?" The barking became more frantic and playful and Tripod's excited whining was joined with urgent scratching on the doorframe. Suddenly the door opened, and Tripod hobbled out as fast as she could.

Terri stood, eyes locked on Sheila's for several seconds before bending over to greet the dog. After a minute of ecstatic canine belly rubbing, Terri straightened. Before she could say anything, Sheila spoke calmly. "I have a few things to say to you." Terri opened her mouth to speak but Sheila stopped her. "No, you listen, the last time you were here, you did most of the talking and left. Over the last two weeks I've had a lot of time to think about the last few months."

Terri rubbed at her chest. Her muscles tensed preparing for the coming harsh words. Swallowing hard against the sudden tightness in her throat her voice cracked. "Can I come inside? Can we do this inside?"

Sheila opened the door further to allow Terri in before closing it completely. She walked into the kitchen, pulled out a new chew toy for the dog and handed it to her. Tripod happily hobbled off to a sunny spot on the kitchen floor. Sheila stood looking across the room to where Terri stood by the fireplace, looking at the pictures she had put on the mantle. Pictures of the two them from their kayaking trip, fitting Tripod with the harness at the clinic, and one of Terri in her studio working.

Sheila waited to speak until Terri turned toward her. "I'm sorry. You were right. At least part of what you said was right. But a good part was wrong, too. I realized while you've been gone that I took too much for granted. I put your needs after mine, consistently. Not only am I truly sorry for that, I am embarrassed by that, too. I've tried to come up with a reason, but no matter what I came up with, it was just an excuse. In some ways I was afraid, in other ways I was so damn glad that you wanted to be with me. My ex had been such an ass, so self-centered that I was glad to finally have someone pay attention to my needs. Unfortunately, I acted like him, I neglected you. I didn't give you the

162

time or the support you needed. I'm so very sorry." Sheila's eyes filled. She wiped her eyes. "But you were wrong, too. You said I was not taking the relationship seriously, and although I was careless, it was serious to me." At Terri's frown she corrected. "Not was, it is important to me. You heard part of my conversation with Peter. Correct me if I'm wrong, you heard me tell Peter that I wasn't going with anyone, right?"

Terri stood, arms across her chest and nodded slightly. "I did."

"He wanted me to go up to Virginia to attend a fundraiser with him. He even offered to fix me up with someone. I refused. I told him I was not going with anyone. That's what you heard, Terri. I was not denying our relationship. I was refusing to spend time with people who are no longer a part of my life. My life is here now, with you. Why didn't you tell me what you heard?"

Terri stood motionless for few seconds and breathed deeply. "It hurt too much to know that..." She took a jagged breath. "That I was being rejected. That my parents were right."

"No, they weren't." Sheila shook her head.

"And then the flowers..."

"We had lunch. That's it. It wasn't a date. I was at the Outfitter for lunch, it was packed. I invited him to sit with me. And yes, I was flattered that a good-looking man was paying attention to me. But, Terri, that was it. I was being friendly, he was letting me know he was interested in more. I'm not. Yes, I found him attractive, but that doesn't mean it was going to progress any further. I was already in a relationship with you. I love you." Sheila watched as Terri's eyes widened and her brows lifted. "Why do you look surprised?"

Terri's eyes filled, and her throat was tight as she tried to control the tears. "I don't think I've ever heard that before."

Sheila nearly jumped across the room, and cupped Terri's face in her hands. "I love you, I'm going to start telling you that more often." She reached up and pulled their mouths together. Her lips touched Terri's once, twice, then drifted across her jaw to kiss and nuzzle where she was sensitive. She smiled when Terri let out a low sensual moan. Gliding her hands across Terri's neck she whispered, "Come upstairs. I want you."

Drawing Terri behind her she led her up to the bedroom. Kissing her delicately, she unbuttoned Terri's shirt, slid it aside, and murmured in her ear, "I've missed you so much." Sliding her hands between them, she unfastened Terri's pants, slid them down and slowly trailed her fingers along her well-muscled legs, feeling little quivers of flesh as she moved on.

She helped Terri step free of her jeans. When Terri turned to kiss her, she stopped her. "Lie down, sweetheart. On your stomach. I'll be right back." She turned down the bedding before guiding Terri onto the bed and stepping away.

***

Terri lay naked on the cool sheets, listening to Sheila move around in the adjoining bath and heard her call out, "How about some music?" Before she could answer, music started, an ethereal wave began to fill the room. The bed gave as Sheila moved up next to her and leaned over. "Relax, hon. I know you're going to like this." The cool slide of silk passed over her face, then around her ears before she realized Sheila's intention, and she jerked. "Shh! Lie still, trust me."

With her heart accelerating, Terri lowered her head as Sheila tied the silk scarf in place, effectively and completely blindfolding her. Weight shifted, and Terri felt her hips pressed between Sheila's firm thighs. Silky panties slid across her bare bottom. Soft, smooth hands stroked up her spine, and Sheila's breasts dragged across her back. "Lie still, enjoy."

Warm liquid oozed across her back, and was swept across her shoulders, neck, and down across her back. The smell of sandalwood filled the air, mixing with the light scent of the trees that drifted in on the slightest breeze from outside.

Hands, strong and sure, slid up her spine, across her shoulders and caressed back down. The stress of the weeks slipped out of her body as the strokes gradually became more intense. Knots of tension dissolved under loving hands. Her arms relaxed under Sheila's loving touch. Sighing, she murmured incomprehensibly as slick, warm hands moved down her flank before settling on the smooth globes of her butt.

Fingers and palms dug in with comfortable pressure, lifting and rolling her cheeks before advancing down her legs. More warm liquid oozed onto her legs, mixing with the pool of her own wetness. Deep strokes along the length of her legs, skillfully found and released knots of tension. Each toe was lovingly caressed and rotated to relieve its tiny load. With a deep sigh Terri drifted under.

She awakened shortly, reached for the blindfold. "No. Leave it. Roll over, sweetheart, we're just getting started." Terri rolled over, warm oil drizzled across her chest. Her breasts swelled, nipples tightening as

Sheila spread the oil across her sensitive flesh. Slick thumbs grazed purposefully across nipples, tweaking them.

Weight settled on her as Sheila lay on top and pressed breast to breast. Terri gasped in surprise as teeth set lightly on her collarbone. She groaned when a hand slipped between her thighs, sliding against her wetness.

"Oh, Ter, you're so wet."

Terri's legs were nudged apart, fingers stroked between her folds, spreading her. Her hips arched in primitive response as fingers teased at her opening before, ever so slowly, penetrating her. She moaned in frustration. "Please, take me."

"I am. I will." The blindfold was pushed away from her eyes, in a few seconds she was able to open them against the seemingly bright light. Fingers stroked smoothly into her, gliding across the sensitive place inside until she was lifting her hips in rhythm with the strokes, desperate for deeper penetration.

"Sheila, please." Strokes increased, hips thrust, breast to breast they moved against each other, mouths locked in a slow sensual kiss.

"Look at me." Panting for breath, hips thrusting, Terri looked into bright hazel eyes, and seeing the intensity in them, she clutched and spasmed as "I love you, Terri" rang in her ears, and her heart nearly exploded.

Terri lay crying softly, wrapped in Sheila's arms, an emotional wreck. Never had she felt so loved, so cared for. So full. Sheila played with the hair along her neck and caressed down her back. After several minutes she regained control of her emotions. She lifted her head and looked at Sheila. "I'm sorry. I don't know what happened."

Sheila placed her fingers across Terri's lips. "Don't apologize. It was beautiful. You're beautiful." They nuzzled against each other, and when Terri's breathing became more stable and her trembling stopped, Sheila once again whispered, "I love you."

Roslyn Bane

Chapter Twenty-seven

SHEILA SMILED, "TERRI, RELAX."

Terri stopped pacing momentarily. "I can't. What if he is just like them?"

"He's not."

"How do you know that? How can you be so sure?" She turned and headed back across the porch, rubbing her hand across the back of her neck.

"He searched for you. Through the years your brother kept searching. You've spoken on the phone several times now. I've spoken to him briefly."

"Yeah, but—"

Sheila stepped behind Terri and started to massage her shoulders. "You're so tense. Come on, Ter. Relax. It'll be all right. You'll see."

Terri turned to face her. "What if it's not?"

Sheila met Terri's eyes. "Then we'll ask them to leave. Turn back around and let me rub your shoulders some more. Your muscles are so tight. Sit down."

Terri lowered herself into a chair. "I think I'm going to be sick."

"No, you won't. You haven't eaten anything today and picked at your dinner last night."

"I haven't seen him since he was in seventh grade. What if he doesn't approve—"

"Stop. Terri, he probably knows you're gay. He was home the night your parents hurt you." Sheila swallowed hard. "The night you had to leave. But if he doesn't know, he soon will. He doesn't have to approve. You didn't need his approval before, and you don't need it now."

"I know but, ohhh." She moaned as Sheila nibbled the sensitive spot on her neck, and fingers stroked along the front of her neck.

Sheila continued to kiss Terri's neck and her hands slid down across Terri's chest, gently cupping and caressing her breasts. "Shh, come on, Ter. Relax. Breathe out."

Terri struggled to swallow and leaned her head back. "Mmm, ah."

She shivered and turned toward Sheila when suddenly Tripod stood and barked. Several seconds later, a minivan appeared and turned into her driveway. She whispered, "They're here."

Terri stood up and took several stiff legged steps toward the steps. Her mouth went dry and her heart stuttered. *What the hell am I going to say to them? We have nothing in common except the ghosts of our pasts. Why did I want this?* Sheila's warm hand in hers refocused her attention. They walked across the yard to where the van parked. Tripod barked softly beside them. A brown-haired woman stepped out of the passenger side of the van. Her belly was round, and she placed her hands in the small of her back and arched. She smiled at Terri, and when her eyes shifted to Sheila and their still held hands, she continued to smile.

"Hi. You must be Marion." Terri stepped forward and offered her hand.

"I am. Terri, it's so nice to finally meet you." She shook Terri's hand. "This must be Sheila?"

"Hi. It's nice to meet you." As they shook hands, a tall man, a few inches above six feet came around the front of the van holding a young child, who had a sleepy look in his eyes. Both had jet-black hair. As a teddy bear fell from the child's arms, Tripod pounced on it.

"No, Tripod," Terri and Sheila commanded together. Tripod sat with the well-loved bear in her mouth. Terri held out her hand and Tripod released the bear into her hand. She wiped the bear off and held it out towards her brother like a talisman. "Stevie?" Her voice broke.

"Hi Terri."

She would never be able to recall exactly what happened, but somehow, she ended up wrapped in her brother's arms. It was several seconds before she realized that they were crying. He hugged her fiercely. "Thank God I found you. Thank you for calling me." He let go and scooped up the boy who was tugging at his pants. "This is Andy. You already met Fuzzy Bear."

Terri wiped tears from her cheeks. "I did. Hi, Andy." The child turned his face into his father's shoulder. Terri's eyes shifted to Sheila and saw her nod her head.

Marion spoke, "It's okay, Andy, Aunt Terri just wants to say hi."

Sheila was introduced to Steve, and pleasantries were exchanged.

Andy pointed a finger and excitedly exclaimed, "Doggie."

"That's right. The doggie's name is Tripod. Would you like to meet her?" Terri asked.

"Yes!"

Steve knelt, placing Andy on his knee, and Terri stood beside them. "Tripod, come."

Tail wagging, Tripod came over.

Sheila came forward with Tripod, as they watched to see how both dog and child would react to each other.

"She has three legs," Marion said.

As Andy giggled and patted Tripod's head Terri told her how she got Tripod and met Sheila. They made their way into the house and as Sheila prepared drinks, Terri showed her family around her home. A short while later they sat outside and caught up with each other. They shared happy moments in their lives. While Terri grilled, Sheila set the table, Andy and Steve tossed a ball with Tripod, who was now in her harness and running about the yard chasing the mangled ball.

Marion rested inside as the trip was long and difficult on her because of her pregnancy. Terri's thoughts wandered as she watched her brother. *I don't know him anymore. He's a man now. He seems loving and kind. Look how he plays with his son. His son, for God sake. He has kids. And loves them. What does that feel like, to have a little person dependent on you? Looking to you for love and protection. For food, for everything. How could he do it and not be afraid that he would hurt the child? And Marion. She's pretty, and huge. I wonder when she's due? I hope she doesn't pop while she's here. She's active, you can tell. Even though she's big with pregnancy her body is still toned. She's loving. Kind. The niceness radiates from her. It's so obvious they love each other.*

"You're going to burn the chicken."

Terri jumped when Sheila 's voice came from behind her. "You startled me." She turned the chicken and started taking skewers of vegetables from the platter that Sheila held and placed them on the grill. She nodded toward her brother, "He looks happy. I was afraid that he would look like my father. He doesn't, not at all. He's taller. More muscular. And his face is nicer. More refined."

Sheila traced her hand on Terri's arm. "Do you feel better now? Not as nervous?"

"Yes. Thank you for being here with me." She kissed Sheila on the forehead.

"I wouldn't dream of not being here for you. Marion is awake. She looks more refreshed. It's been a fun but long trip for them. They visited Marion's family in DC and spent a few days in Nags Head. They planned on stopping at the zoo in Asheboro yesterday, but it was raining."

"Aunt Terri, I hungry."

Terri scooped the little boy up and smiled broadly. "You are? Well that's good news because dinner is ready. Do you like chicken?"

"Yes. Beans and corn. I like cookies. Can we have cookies?"

"I don't think we can have cookies for dinner. Maybe after dinner if your dad says it's okay."

Steve laughed and took Andy from Terri. "Of course, we can have cookies. Let's go wash our hands and get Mommy."

A few minutes later they were all seated around the table. They enjoyed the meal outside and after a quick cleanup Sheila took Marion and Andy to a nearby playground. Terri and Steve sat on the front porch, and after a few minutes of silence Terri spoke first. "Stevie, I'm sorry I left you. I came back. But you were gone. All your things were, too."

"Terri, you didn't leave me. You escaped." Steve reached out and took Terri's hand. He stroked his fingers over the scar on the back of her hand. "You got this that night. You have others, don't you?"

Terri gasped. "I...I do."

"I saw what they did. I was afraid and hid. I should have helped you, I should have tried to stop them."

Terri vigorously shook her head. "No Stevie. There's nothing you could have done."

"I should have called the police. I have kicked myself so many times for not calling for help."

Terri took his hand in hers and held it firmly, "No. They had us afraid of the police. Damn, Stevie they had us afraid of just about everyone who could have helped us." She wiped at the tears that were on his cheeks. "I came back to get you, but you were gone. They told me you were safe and in foster care, so I took off and headed south. I was in Roanoke for a few years, then Charlotte. I eventually made it here. Things got better for you, right?"

"When I was in my first foster home, things were good. But that home was for short-term placement. It was sort of a rescue house. After two weeks I was placed with another family, they were strict and very religious. I started having nightmares. Their church reminded me of the one we went to. Hellfire and brimstone type. When the preacher started preaching about 'spare the rod and spoil the child' I ran away. They sent me back. There were daily bible readings and strict chores. Punishments. I ran away again and again. Eventually, someone listened, and I was placed in a home with no males. I was lucky. They placed me with an older lesbian couple. I'm not sure how that happened, given the time, but I thank God for it. They treated me well, nurtured me. Gave me love. I had started to bully younger kids at school. They set rules and wouldn't tolerate the behavior. Eventually I broke down and told them that I hadn't helped you. I told them what I had heard shouted at you that night. They got me help. They helped me to understand that love and unfortunately hate comes in all shapes and sizes. They saved my life."

"Do you still see them?"

"Yes. They encouraged me to look for you and were thrilled when I found you. Andy calls them both Gramma."

"That's good. You have a wonderful family. When is Marion due?"

"Eight more weeks. Terri, tell me more about your life."

"Stevie...Can, I call you Steve?" He nodded. "I travel a lot as a photographer. I found this place a few years back. Well, it was a lot smaller. I pretty much tore the old cabin down. Remodeled and rebuilt it. I bought it as a getaway, but it became home. Sheila lives nearby. I never thought I would meet someone. Trust someone. But I do. Does it make sense if I say she has helped me to heal?"

"It does. I'm happy for you."

They both looked over as Sheila's truck pulled back into the driveway, the sound of laughter coming out of the open windows.

***

Marion and Sheila sat outside on the porch as the sun went down. The sound of childish laughter could be heard inside the house. Terri and Steve's laughter joined in.

"The laughter sounds nice. I'm so glad you were able to come down and visit. This has been a very good day."

"It has. I don't mind telling you that Steve was very nervous. I thought I was going to have to drive the last few miles. He was almost shaking."

Sheila smiled. "Terri was too. I thought she was going to pass out. I think this visit is going to help her."

"I know it will help Steve. It's been a long time coming. He has searched for so long. Even though we work with abused children daily, and he has a therapist, it was necessary that he try to meet with Terri. He was afraid that she would want nothing to do with him. That it would bring up bad memories."

"Terri was afraid that Steve would hate her because she left him alone with them."

Marion shook her head and raised her hand to her chest, "Oh God, no. He understood back then, and certainly does now."

"She was also afraid he would reject her because she's homosexual."

"He knew. In one of the early conversations we had back when we were dating, he mentioned Terri, and said she was. He remembered his parent's angry conversations about it."

"I've never asked Terri how her parents found out she was gay. Given the abuse I don't think she would have told them."

"Steve and I discussed this. He found out that during the trial—"

Sheila raised an eyebrow. "Trial?"

"After Steve was removed from the home and Terri disappeared there was an investigation. Although Terri couldn't be found, apparently the school nurse had taken pictures of Terri's back and that was shown in court. There was also other testimony from teachers, through the years, who said that both of them always seemed to have bruises. It turns out the guidance counselor at the high school had seen Terri leaving the movie theater one night with a girl and holding her hand. The counselor went to the same church as their parents and told them."

"Oh, God."

"Yes, she wanted them to know that Terri was a sinner. You can imagine how I feel about that."

Sheila stood up and paced. "That's just unbelievable. What right did that woman have to do that?"

"She didn't. It gets worse. She followed Terri around the school and saw her and this girl having close conversations." Marion used her fingers to put air quotes around close conversations.

"That's just bullshit."

"Exactly. I can tell you that's what the school board thought, too. It's little consolation but I can tell you, she was fired."

"Good. Where are their parents now?"

"Their father died in prison when it got around that he abused his children, he was beaten to death."

Sheila chewed on her lip as she processed the information. "Where's their mother?"

"When she got out of prison, she was placed in a half-way house. She was on parole and eventually released from there. We're not sure where she is. The last we were able to find out was she was in Texas three years ago. She wasn't in good health, so she may not be alive."

Sheila stared out across the lawn before speaking. "I don't know that I am sorry about that. I hope that doesn't bother you."

"Not at all. There are times that I still want to give that woman a butt kicking. I like to think she will get what's due to her."

"Amen."

They stopped talking to watch as Tripod pushed open the screen door and plopped down between them. Marion reached down and pet Tripod's head. "She's a good dog. Is she yours or Terri's?"

Sheila laughed. "Well technically she is Terri's. I take care of her when Terri travels."

"May I ask how long you two have been together?"

"Since the spring."

"It's obvious you both care deeply for each other."

"I love her."

Marion smiled. "Good. Can I give you some advice?" Sheila nodded. "Many people who were abused the way Terri and Steve were have a hard time with relationships. They have a tendency to pull back when things get intense. And not just intense in a bad way. Even when things appear to be going well, they often will withdraw. Many don't believe, deep down, that they deserve happiness. So, they withdraw or push others away to avoid getting hurt. For some, when they feel deeply, it results in fear. You have to be patient and realize that as children they would have tried hard to be invisible. To be seen or heard risked drawing attention and attention was seldom good. I'm telling you this because you need to be aware of this and decide what you're willing to do to stay with her."

"Did Steve have this problem?"

"Oh, yes. We've been to counseling together and he has gone by himself. I occasionally must point out to him when he is doing it, but he is usually aware of it. It took a long while to get there. We dated for five years before we married, and there were lots of rough spots in there. Counseling helped us."

"Terri hasn't been to counseling, at least as far as I know. I've encouraged her too, but I know I can't force her."

"No, you can't."

Their conversation was interrupted when Terri emerged from the house carrying Andy, freshly bathed and in Thomas the Tank Engine pajamas. Sheila pressed her hand to her stomach when it hitched.

Andy's jet-black hair stood up in spikes like Terri's. The boy was beaming at Terri and offering her a bite of the cookie clutched in his chubby hand. Laughing she took a little nibble of the treat. It left Sheila feeling flustered and warm to see their interaction. A moment later the spell was broken when Andy saw his mom and reached for her.

Terri put him down, "I see how you are, pushing me aside for another girl." She laughed. "Anyone need anything to drink? Steve is cleaning up the bathroom. Apparently, there was a tidal wave in there."

Everyone answered they were fine, so Terri settled down in a rocking chair. Andy climbed up into her lap and as the adults talked, he fell asleep in her lap. Several minutes later Steve joined them, and they discussed their plans for the next day, including taking a train ride on a steam engine that was sure to keep Andy entertained. A short while later their guests left to return to their hotel room.

***

The next morning, they met at the historic train depot in Bryson City. As the steam engine rounded the corner, it blew its whistle and steam poured from the chimney, Andy shrieked with delight. By the time they took their seats on the train, Andy was trembling with excitement. As the train started to move, Terri was able to capture the enchanted look on his face. Over the next few hours they enjoyed the ride as it took them along the Nantahala and Tennessee rivers. The beautiful scenery of the gorge spread out before them. Terri gave them a short history lesson about the area and took photos of their trip. They enjoyed lunch at the Nantahala Outdoor Center, watching as whitewater rafts and kayakers paddled by on the river. They enjoyed dinner together at Natasha's before retiring early after the busy day.

***

Before the final hugs goodbye, Steve and Terri stood off to the side. "It means a lot to me that you let us come down and visit you, Terri. I know it was a short visit, but it means so much. It's good to know that you are well." He glanced over at Sheila. "She loves you. The way she looks at you, the way her body changes when she sees you. It says love all over her. Accept her love, Terri, it's a gift. We were brought up not to expect love, but it's standing right in front of you, in the form of Sheila. Accept it and give it back. At first, I had a hard time returning Marion's love, I was afraid to. It will be worth it." He hugged Terri, picked her up and spun around with her twice. Terri shrieked, and Andy burst into laughter. "Now please promise me that you will visit us."

"I will. We will."

Terri and Sheila hugged everyone again and they stood arm in arm, watching as they drove away.

Roslyn Bane

Chapter Twenty-eight

SHEILA AWOKE TO THE aroma of coffee. She slipped into a robe and walked to the kitchen, not surprised when she didn't see Terri or her camera. She filled a cup, added a splash of cream, sipped and enjoyed the dark blend. She sighed when that first hit of caffeine started to awaken her.

Picking up a magazine, she headed out to the deck, and took several deep breaths of the late September morning air. A hint of wood smoke lingered in the breeze and reminded her Fall was coming. She startled when she saw Terri leaning against the railing. She walked up slowly, wrapped her arms around Terri's waist, and felt her jump in surprise. Sheila nuzzled behind her ear.

"Good morning."

"Morning." Terri leaned back, relaxing again, tipping her head to the side to enjoy the soft nibbles.

"What are you looking at?"

"The clouds."

Sheila stopped nuzzling, looked up, and watched the clouds build in wispy tendrils then immediately drift and reform. "When I see them like that, it reminds me of you."

"Of me?" Terri turned. "What, like Eeyore?"

Sheila snorted with laughter, and swatted Terri on the arm. "Stop it. You have one of the best dispositions of anyone I know. I meant the clouds, they're always moving, drifting, mysterious as they move up the mountain." When Terri tried to interrupt, Sheila placed a finger across her lips. "Let me finish. If you're willing to wait, those mysterious clouds will part and leave you looking at some sweet surprise that you've never seen before, that you could never have imagined. It leaves you breathless." Sheila reached up and guided Terri's mouth to hers. "Baby, you are no Eeyore." The embrace ended, and Sheila took Terri's hand to lead her across the deck. "Come back inside."

"Wait a minute." They faced each other. Terri tucked some hair behind Sheila's ear and then grasped both of her hands. "I never thought I would be here. Like this. In some dark crazy way, I'm here because of the terrible things my parents did to me. I didn't deserve it, no one does. But what happened set me on a path and it led me here, and I found you. I would never trade a single moment of that if it would change the way things are now. I love you." Terri's hands moved to Sheila's waist, holding her gently, and kissed her. "I feel so alive with you."

Sheila smiled, laughed, and wrapped her arms around Terri's shoulders. "I love you, too. I can't wait anymore. Move in with me, love. You and Tripod come live with me."

With tears in her eyes and the dog nudging against their legs, Terri smiled. "Yes. Yes, we will."

The End

If you or a loved one are an adult survivor of child abuse and are in need of assistance, please contact the National Association of Adult Survivors of Child Abuse. www.naasca.org

About Roslyn Bane

Roslyn Bane, contemporary romance author of LGBT romances, filled with love, friendship and small towns.

Roslyn Bane wrote poetry and short stories in high school which remained largely unseen except by her closest friends. She grew up in Maryland and lived in the Florida panhandle, coastal Virginia and Wisconsin before settling near York, Pennsylvania.

Her inspiration for stories comes from daily life, hobbies, her love of the outdoors, and people watching.

Connect with Roslyn at:

Email: rojodek@outlook.com
Facebook: Roslyn Bane

Excerpt from The Last Line of Defense. Book Two in the Smoky Mountain Romance series.

Last Line of Defense

Working with precision, Malachai wrapped the bundles of pine straw with 3 pieces of twine, each 6 inches long. Mumbling while working "Six times three is eighteen and on the 38th day the first king shall come for the offering. Luke will come to cast the fire, let us prepare the funeral pyre."

Over and over Malachai repeated the phrase, as each of the 209 bundles of pine needles, as thick as two fingers, were tied tightly and placed on the creamy white cloth that once adorned the altar at Saint Elizabeth's Church in Norman, Oklahoma. After the last bundle was placed upon the cloth Malachai stood, and folded the cloth into a neat bundle, bowed and kissed it.

Striding across the deeply rutted patch of grass that passed for a lawn, Malachai moved to the ancient propane tank. Attaching the tank hose to the fish fryer purchased at the Great Bargains Store, the Lord's Prayer came to mind and was said out loud before the aluminum fry pot was placed on the cooking stand. Malachi removed the plastic tarp from over the wheelbarrow and poured three gallons of water into the fry pot.

Malachi opened the valve on the propane tank, looked away, and pushed the button on the electronic igniter. The whoosh as the fuel lit sent a shudder through Malachai's body. Mal smiled as the warmth penetrated the dirty canvas jacket and carpenter jeans. Refocusing on the task at hand, Mal placed five one-pound blocks of paraffin wax into a smaller vessel and placed it into the pot of simmering water. When the wax started to melt Malachai smiled, causing the cleft in the chin to deepen, and hurried back to the picnic table and laid hands upon the bundle.

"Now the servants and officers had made a charcoal fire, because it was cold, and they were warming themselves." Malachai lifted the bundle and returned to the fish fryer. The bundle was placed in the wheelbarrow and opened. Mal pulled a pair of tongs from the side pocket of the carpenter jeans, lifted a bundle of pine straw, kissed it, placed it between the tong blades and plunged it into the melted wax for three seconds. "Six times three is eighteen, and on the 38th day the first king shall come for the offering. Luke will come to cast the fire, let us prepare the funeral pyre."

An hour later as the last waxy bundled cooled Malachai tenderly picked up the first bundles, kissed each again and wrapped them once more in the creamy white cloth. The sun was low in the sky when the last bundle of pine straw was placed, and the cloth was reverently folded. Malachai dissembled the fish fryer, drug the propane tank back into the woods, and placed it back in the crumbling wood shed. Kicking over the water pots Malachai pulled on wool gloves, lifted the two pots, and threw them into the woods, one to the east and one to the west, for the land in between was fertile.

Malachai marched back to the picnic table, placed the bundle into the backpack, and struck out along the path heading down the mountain. After several hours the temple was found. Malachai removed the pack, and with great care opened the bundle. Sticking to the shadows, Mal approached the back of the temple of the Minit Market, pulled trash from the dumpster, and spread it against the back of the building.

Placing the pack over the right shoulder, closest to the hand of God, Mal placed several bundles of the pine straw into the heap of trash and moving backward, positioned the pine straw bundles end to end across the parking lot and out into the woods. Avoiding the path and moving through the dry underbrush, each bundle was placed into piles of leaves.

The night animals in the woods grew silent as Malachai worked. At 11:50 p.m. Mal found the creek, stripped and climbed into the cool crisp water. "With water I baptize you, but someone else shall come later and baptize you with fire."

By 11:59 Malachai stood fully clothed, heart racing, warmth spreading through the temple of the body. Mal pulled a match from a pocket and admired it. The flame hissed to life as the match scratched against his pants zipper. After two seconds Malachai bent and placed the match against the bundle of pine straw. A bright flare of light and burst of heat as the straw ignited momentarily paralyzed Mal, before a lick of fire raced out to touch the next bundle of straw.

Mal ignored the tingle of excitement, picked up the pack, stepped into the water, and ran downstream. Emerging from the water several minutes later, Mal looked back to see the orange glow in the sky. Opening the pants fly, Malachai reached inside, stroked quickly, and cried out the orgasm as the boom of the gas station exploding obliterated the silence of the night.

Available 2019

Note to Readers:

Thank you for reading a book from Desert Palm Press. We have made every effort to edit this book. However, typos do slip in. If you find an error in the text, please email lee@desertpalmpress.com so the issue can be corrected.

We appreciate you as a reader and want to ensure you enjoy the reading process. We would like you to consider posting a review on your preferred media sites and/or your blog or website.

For more information on upcoming releases, author interviews, contest, giveaways and more, please sign up for our newsletter and visit us as at Desert Palm Press: www.desertpalmpress.com and "Like" us on Facebook: Desert Palm Press.

Bright Blessing

www.ingramcontent.com/pod-product-compliance
Lightning Source LLC
Chambersburg PA
CBHW051121260626
47170CB00005B/1609